9. Thus passed 20 mos.
the "idea" seems to be placed above the action.

11 knowing the blessing of hope, Rasselas
would never despair

14 knows (morn, evening & night)

15 in a year

19 Imlac's youth serves as a foil to Rasselas
(20)

26 Truth will be found where it is honestly sought.

SAMUEL JOHNSON

27 Life is to be endured — not be enjoyed.

37 spies in Cairo

38 Imlac: "happiness is not to be found", Rasselas, "I must
find happiness"

The History

of Rasselas

Prince Of Abyssinia

very little character portrayal or development

40 - recovers his tranquility & continues search
(flat character novel)

42 - archetypal - moralist / death figure

43 - still eager upon the same enquiry

(45 - went to find hermit

46. hermit "just happened" to be going back
to civilization when Rasselas got there.
(no evil, but no place for virtue)

60 only thing that comes to point of view
is socratic dialogue.

61. Marriage needs reason.

69. Pyramid as folly.

73. virtue is never repented.

84 angels of affliction

Crofts Classics

GENERAL EDITORS

Samuel H. Beer, *Harvard University*

O. B. Hardison, Jr., *The Folger Shakespeare Library*

John Simon

84. the captives of the Arabs, brew coffee & had few ideas.

87. Prince to devote himself to learning

92. The astronomer & fear of the loss of reason

95. anti-imagination (the fantasies of the three characters

97. Old Man's hope after death.

97. Imlac forbears telling them of friendship

102. Imagination & deity really secretive

103. Life of reason & deity, with thoughts on the after-life is most suitable

Instruction on immortality of soul.

SAMUEL JOHNSON

The History
of Rasselas
Prince of Abyssinia

EDITED BY

Gwin J. Kolb

UNIVERSITY OF CHICAGO

APPLETON-CENTURY-CROFTS

Educational Division

New York MEREDITH CORPORATION

Copyright © 1962 by

MEREDITH CORPORATION

All rights reserved

7110-6

390-22655-6

INTRODUCTION

THOUGH JOHNSON had long entertained the principal views expressed in the work, the immediate cause of *Rasselas* seems to have been the death of his mother in January of 1759, at the ripe age of 90. In the *Life*, Boswell reports, on good authority, that Johnson wrote the tale in order to "defray the expence of" the "funeral" and to "pay some little debts . . . left" by his mother. Boswell continues: "He [Johnson] told Sir Joshua Reynolds that he composed it in the evenings of one week, sent it to the press in portions as it was written, and had never since read it over." Three outstanding London booksellers—Robert Dodsley, William Johnston, and William Strahan—were the joint proprietors of the book; and one of the three—Strahan—was also the printer. The owners paid Johnson £ 100 for the first edition, £ 25 for the second. *Rasselas* was published in two volumes octavo on April 19, 1759; a second edition, which, his supposed remark to Sir Joshua Reynolds notwithstanding, Johnson lightly revised, appeared on June 26 of the same year. The total number of editions published between 1759 and 1962 must run to well over 450; and, as the present edition demonstrates, the end is not even remotely in sight.

Like many other artistic creations, *Rasselas* has been interpreted in several different ways. An early reviewer, for example, warning prospective readers not to be misled by the title and insisting that "*tale-telling* is not the talent" of the author, compared Johnson's book unfavorably with conventional "oriental" romances of the sort exemplified by the *Arabian Nights*. A number of literary historians, while acknowledging a fundamental distinction between the work and the ordinary novel, still feel compelled to measure *Rasselas* in terms (e.g., unity of action, element of suspense, dramatic quality of the characters, etc.) usually applied to novelistic structures and techniques. Within the past decade, two critics have argued that the tale can be read as a "comedy," although one commentator mentions the likeness between *Rasselas* and Johnson's intensely serious poem *The Vanity of Human Wishes,* and the other points out a marked "darkening" of the comedy in the latter part of the book.

Each of these interpretations performs a useful service by emphasizing salient features of Johnson's work. The tale *does* contain such standard trappings of the oriental romance as an exotic setting, highborn personages of both sexes, hidden identities, stories within the frame story, and a (mildly) exciting adventure—the abduction and return of the maid of honor, Pekuah. Like a typical novel, it also consists of a longish narrative in which a group of characters, who possess definite personalities, begin, continue, and finally conclude a series of actions. And, though its effects are seldom purely comic, the book includes a moderate range of amusing passages as well as several episodes wherein various characters, the hero among them, are made to appear ridiculous.

But even a hasty examination of *Rasselas* is enough to convince the new reader that neither *oriental romance* nor *novel* nor *comedy* adequately describes the contents and organization of what, judged by both number of editions and critical acclaim, is a manifest literary masterpiece. From the opening sentence through the last chapter, the problem of happiness—its relation to human nature and the external world—emerges as the main concern of the work and the chief determinant by reference to which questions concerning its structure may be most fruitfully answered. *Rasselas* may therefore, in accordance with the classification used by many commentators, be labelled a moral tale or apologue, a common *genre* in eighteenth-century literature; and the story of the prince and his companions may be considered a vehicle for presenting to the reader certain notions about happiness and for inculcating in him specific attitudes with respect to the human condition. Briefly stated, the "lesson" of the book runs something like this: Man's nature—the insatiable "hunger" of his "imagination"—and the nature of the world produce at best only a scanty amount of happiness, which is often accidental, never lasting, and insignificant when balanced against the predominant bleakness of life. Mindful of his own limitations, the wise person will thus recognize the futility of searches for permanent felicity (although such searches are almost inevitable to man as man), ask no more of life than virtuous conduct can provide, and look to eternity and to God's mercy for the pure bliss that is unattainable on earth.

Before writing *Rasselas*, Johnson had composed two works, *The Vanity of Human Wishes* (an "imitation" of Juvenal's Tenth Satire) and *Rambler* papers 204-05, setting forth similar views of human life and urging a similar moral on the audience. In the *Rambler* papers, furthermore, he employed for the conveyance of his instruction the story of Seged, King of Abyssinia, who, resolving to be completely happy for ten days, withdraws to an island paradise where he practices, without success, various schemes designed to create happiness until the illness of his daughter on the eighth day puts an end to his plans. When he decided to write a third piece embodying the same general theme, Johnson again selected a narrative as his basic device and a member of Abyssinian royalty as his principal character. But whereas Seged in the *Rambler* moves from the ordinary world to a secluded island in pursuit of contentment, Rasselas proceeds in the opposite direction, from a secluded valley to the everyday world, in his vain search for his heart's desire.

Lasting happiness has often, perhaps most frequently, been equated with life in a distant, exotic paradise— witness the appeal of a Pacific island or a Shangri-La in our own time—and the depiction, at the beginning of *Rasselas*, of man's *un*happiness in precisely such a location forms an impressive contribution to Johnson's thesis regarding the paucity of earthly felicity. For assorted details of the Abyssinian setting Johnson was probably indebted to Father Jerome Lobo's *Voyage to Abyssinia*, which he had translated from French into English in 1733. Lobo contains several allusions, for example, to "*Rassela Christos*," identified as "Lieutenant General to *Sultan Segued*"; and it also refers to the ancient policy of confining, for purposes of political stability, male relations of the Abyssinian emperor until the order of succession should elevate them to the throne. But Lobo's grim and essentially accurate description of the royal prison—a "Barren summit" of a rock in the kingdom of Amhara, where the princes "pass'd" "melancholy" lives—obviously has little in common with the delights of the "happy valley" in *Rasselas,* which owes its conception to a romantic tradition that was widespread during the seventeenth and eighteenth centuries. According to this charming fantasy (found in *Purchas His Pilgrimage* [1613], among other travel books), the royal retreat was a veritable terrestrial paradise, graced with such appropriate features as a delicious climate, lovely lake, luxuriant gardens, harmless animals and beautiful birds, magnificent palaces, rich treasury and great library, and grave instructors who taught diverse subjects to their noble charges. In his employment of the fanciful legend, Johnson, it is worth noting, was following the lead of Milton in *Paradise Lost* and James Thomson in *The Seasons,* and anticipating Coleridge's later use of it in *Kubla Khan.*

The first part of Rasselas gradually reveals the absence of lasting happiness, and the preponderance of discontent, in the paradisaical "happy valley." Part two discloses the same condition in the ordinary world. Since the only remaining locale with respect to happiness would be a spot completely deficient in means to pleasure—a spot in which perhaps no one could imagine happiness possible—these two parts achieve, in effect, an exhaustive survey of the varieties of places where happiness might be discovered.

We are introduced to the prince of Abyssinia in the second chapter. Rasselas is a young man in his twenty-sixth year, well past the age when the sheer novelty of the world suffices to make life pleasant and interesting, whose character as a serious, high-minded, dissatisfied, rather naive individual is eminently adapted to the functioning of the apologue. Bored with the luxuries of the valley, he recognizes that the proper happiness of man differs from animal contentment, and he regrets his lack of this happiness. His attempt to obtain it by finding a person who can tell him the recipe for permanent felicity makes up the principal "story" in the book. The record of his thoughts and actions (including encounters with other characters) in Chapters III-VI serves to generate the narrative and also to elaborate Johnson's notions regarding the limited quantity and fleeting quality of happiness.

After trying and eliminating possible avenues of escape from the valley, Rasselas meets the poet Imlac, the most important propounder of the thesis of the tale and inferior only to the prince himself as an agent in the over-all action. Imlac's autobiography, besides showing him to be a person clever enough to effect an escape from the prison and experienced enough to direct Rasselas in his choice of life, contributes materially to the case Johnson is making against faith in earthly happiness. To begin with, it is the history of a more versatile Rasselas, grown mature and wise—but not happy—who may be said to have ended his search for bliss where the younger Rasselas begins his. Secondly, Imlac's account exhibits the final and most comprehensive view of the world's unhappiness painted for Rasselas while he is yet in the valley; "Human life," the poet generalizes, "is everywhere a state in which much is to be endured, and little to be enjoyed." Again, Imlac's remarks regarding felicity in the royal prison expands the number of miserable souls to encompass nearly all the inhabitants. And lastly, the history embroiders the general "lesson" of the book by constantly reminding us that, although an interpolated narrative like those making up a conventional oriental tale, it has nothing to do with the exciting adventures, beautiful women, romance, and happy conclusions characteristic of eastern tales.

In the next three chapters (XIII-XV) of the work, Rasselas and Imlac discover the means of escape from the prison, tunnel through the mountain, and are joined by Nekayah and her favorite, Pekuah. By the addition of the women to the party, Johnson achieves a group whose members represent all the inhabitants of the valley: prince and princess, male and female subordinates—the list is complete. Their willingness to leave offers weighty testimony to the discontent prevailing there. As types, too, the four provide inclusive modes for sampling and commenting on the varieties of life in the ordinary world— the wise Imlac to direct the search and interpret the findings, the naive prince to be gradually disillusioned as he pursues the will-o'-the-wisp of happiness, and Nekayah and the maid of honor for investigations into the distaff domain.

Settled at Cairo, in which he can "see all the conditions of humanity," the prince, heedless of Imlac's cautionary remarks, resolves to examine various states of life with the intention of making a choice for himself. He begins by testing two extreme—and opposing—paths to happiness, one below, the second above, the level on which human beings are capable of sustained pleasure. Mere gratification of sensual appetites cannot be called human happiness because it fails to satisfy peculiarly human capacities; stoicism, on the other hand, with its insistence on the suppression of passions, aims at an elevation of contentment beyond the reach of men as men. Next, moving from the city to the country (another case of procedure by division), Rasselas and his companions inquire into three modes of rural life—those followed by the ignorant, envious shepherds, the cultivated rich man, and the military hermit—that seem at a distance to promise lasting felicity. Like the previous conditions investigated, these variations on supposed bucolic bliss form, by comparison and contrast, a rather orderly treatment designed to impress upon the reader the futility of the "prescription" approach to human pleasure. Back in Cairo again, the prince explores the last of the series of special formulas for happiness. From nature's "philosopher," however, he cannot begin to learn the secret of contentment. The schemes inspected earlier possessed at least the virtue of intelligibility, but the glib advice to cooperate with the present system and be happy lacks even this minor asset.

Chapters XXIII-XXVIII contain a different kind of survey, although directed to the same end as the preceding scrutiny of special recipes for happiness. Rasselas and Nekayah decide to look into "the private recesses of domestic life." Eliminating "low" stations, where "ease" could scarcely be found, they concentrate their examination on "high" and middle conditions. Once again, it should be pointed out, Johnson has achieved a completeness in approach which, viewed in relation to his purpose, can hardly be called accidental. After a vain search for a happy person in "courts" and "private houses," the prince and princess discuss the results of their investigations. Their conversation consists of a discourse on the evils incident to "greatness" and private life, broken up between brother and sister, whose roles shift back and forth from that of a lecturer to that of a listener who, by comments and questions, serves to vary and guide the other's speech. Through it all, the moral of the book is stressed, elaborated, and extended: neither in high stations or moderate, married or single life, youthful or late marriages, nor in virtuous conduct can one hope to discover a full measure of happiness.

With the areas for pure observation pretty well explored, Rasselas and his party become more active agents by taking a trip to the pyramids (themselves eloquent "monument[s] of the insufficiency of human enjoyments"), which results in Pekuah's kidnapping and Nekayah's sorrow. The circumstances of the abduction comprise an impressive example of the dictum, expressed previously by Nekayah, that a virtuous life is not always a happy one; and they also afford Imlac an opportunity of commenting on the "present" and "future" rewards of virtuous behavior. The "progress" of Nekayah's grief discloses her illogical but human tendency to think that change of place will decrease her misery, as well as her gradual, and inevitable, return to the ordinary world. Finally, Pekuah's account of her adventures among the Arabs, besides puncturing (like Imlac's autobiography) "romantic" aspects of the typical oriental tale, enables Johnson to document his thesis concerning happiness by reference to a sphere hitherto unexamined—the life of a sheik and of his harem (representing, in a sense, the reverse of marriage, discussed earlier by Rasselas and Nekayah).

The history of the mad astronomer in Chapters XL-XLIII and the old man's remarks in Chapter XLV bring Rasselas to a terminal point in his search for the best choice of life. Although it is apparently removed from the woes of the world, a life of learning offers no more hope for permanent happiness than the other conditions he has surveyed. Indeed, it may number among its evils the worst of misfortunes—loss of one's sanity; for, the prince discovers, the exercise of the mind itself, the indulgence of the imagination to compensate for the deficiencies of reality, may eventually prevent a person from enjoying any happiness. Nor does the melancholic backward glance of old age hold out to the still optimistic Rasselas (who began his investigations with "young men of spirit") any solid assurance for contentment during his declining years.

In the concluding chapters of the book, Johnson develops the positive side of his argument, i.e., the prospect of eternal happiness, which has been mentioned previously by Nekayah, Imlac, and the old man. Imlac's observations on the "new topic," the life of the monks of St. Anthony, ends with a comparison between our present "transient and probatory" "state" and "the state of future perfection," where "there will be pleasure without danger and security without restraint." And a short time later, in the catacombs, the poet argues strongly for the immateriality—hence natural immortality—of the soul. Nekayah's reaction to the discourse points up Johnson's moral and brings the *History of Rasselas* to a close: "To me," she says, "the choice of life is become less important; I hope hereafter to think only on the choice of eternity." Being young, she, Pekuah, and the prince continue to entertain schemes of happiness, but they know that their wishes cannot "be obtained" and so they decide "to return to Abyssinia." Their decision is at once a sign of the enduring human desire for change in life and, more significant, persuasive evidence of the futility of searches for lasting happiness on earth.

Portions of the Introduction above are drawn from my two essays listed in the Bibliography (p. 112) at the end of this volume. The text of *Rasselas* is that of the first edition, silently corrected in a few places, slightly modernized in spelling and punctuation, and altered to include Johnson's revisions in the second edition (1759) of the work. The explanatory notes rely heavily on definitions in the first edition of Johnson's *Dictionary*, cited thus: "(*Dictionary*)."

THE PRINCIPAL DATES IN THE LIFE
OF SAMUEL JOHNSON

1709 Samuel Johnson born on September 18 at Lichfield in Staffordshire, the son of Michael Johnson, a bookseller, and his wife Sarah.

1717-25 Attended the Lichfield Grammar School, of which "cruel" John Hunter was headmaster.

1725-26 Visited his cousin Cornelius Ford in Stourbridge, Worcestershire; attended Stourbridge Grammar School.

1728 Entered (October 31) Pembroke College, Oxford, as a commoner.

1729 Left (about December 12) Oxford without a degree.

1731 His father died (early December).

1732 Appointed (March) usher at the Grammar School in Market Bosworth, Leicestershire; resigned post in July.

1735 His first book (a translation of Father Jerome Lobo's *Voyage to Abyssinia*) appeared (early in the year); married (July 9) Mrs. Elizabeth ("Tetty") Porter, 45, widow of a Birmingham mercer.

1735 or early 1736 Opened a boarding school at Edial, near Lichfield, with not more than eight pupils, among them David Garrick.

1737 Went (March 2) to London with Garrick; worked on his tragedy *Irene*; settled his wife in London in late autumn.

1738   Began (March) to write for Edward Cave's *Gentleman's Magazine*; published (May 13) *London, a Poem, in Imitation of the Third Satire of Juvenal.*

1741-44   Wrote the Parliamentary Debates for the *Gentleman's Magazine*; published (February 11, 1744) *An Account of the Life of Mr. Richard Savage.*

1747   Published (August) *The Plan of a Dictionary of the English Language,* which was addressed to Philip Dormer Stanhope, Earl of Chesterfield.

1749   Published (January 9) *The Vanity of Human Wishes,* an "imitation" of Juvenal's Tenth Satire; his drama *Irene: A Tragedy* produced (on February 6 and eight succeeding nights) by David Garrick at Drury Lane and published (February 16) shortly thereafter.

1750-52   Wrote and published (from March 20, 1750, to March 14, 1752) *The Rambler* (appearing twice weekly in 208 numbers, of which Johnson was the author of all except four and parts of three others); his wife died (March 28, 1752).

1753-54   Wrote about 30 essays for *The Adventurer,* which appeared twice weekly in 140 numbers from November 7, 1752, to March 9, 1754.

1755   Wrote (early February) the celebrated letter to Lord Chesterfield; published (April 15) *A Dictionary of the English Language.*

1756   Published (June 1) his *Proposals for Printing, by Subscription, the Dramatick Works of Shakespeare.*

1758-60   Wrote *The Idler,* a series of 104 essays (of which Johnson was the author of all except twelve) appearing in the *Universal Chronicle,* a weekly newspaper, from April 15, 1758, to April 5, 1760; his mother died (late January, 1759); published (April 19, 1759) *Rasselas.*

1762 Granted (spring) a pension of 300 pounds a year by George III.

1763 First met (May 16) his biographer James Boswell in the "back-parlour" of Thomas Davies's shop in London.

1764-65 In association with Sir Joshua Reynolds, Edmund Burke, Oliver Goldsmith, and five other men, founded (early 1764) The Club; met (late 1764 or early 1765) Henry Thrale and his wife Hester Lynch Thrale; published (October 10, 1765) *The Plays of William Shakespeare.*

1770 Published (January 16) *The False Alarm.*

1773 Toured (August to November) Scotland and the Hebrides with Boswell.

1775 Published (January 18) *A Journey to the Western Islands of Scotland* and (March 8) *Taxation No Tyranny;* awarded (March 30) the degree of Doctor in Civil Law by Oxford University.

1779-81 Published *Prefaces, Biographical and Critical, to the Works of the English Poets* (i.e., the *Lives of the Poets*), the first four volumes appearing in the spring of 1779, the last six on May 18, 1781.

1784 Died (December 13) at No. 8, Bolt Court, London; buried (December 20) in Westminster Abbey.

THE HISTORY OF RASSELAS

PRINCE OF ABYSSINIA

Description of plenty
"all", "every".

CHAPTER I

DESCRIPTION OF A PALACE IN A VALLEY

Ye who listen with credulity to the whispers of fancy, and pursue with eagerness the phantoms of hope; who expect that age will perform the promises of youth, and that the deficiencies of the present day will be supplied by the morrow; attend to the history of Rasselas[1] prince of Abyssinia.

Rasselas was the fourth son of the mighty emperor in whose dominions the Father of waters[2] begins his course; whose bounty pours down the streams of plenty, and scatters over half the world the harvests of Egypt.

According to the custom[3] which has descended from age to age among the monarchs of the torrid zone, Rasselas was confined in a private palace, with the other sons and daughters of Abyssinian royalty, till the order of succession should call him to the throne.

The place which the wisdom or policy of antiquity had destined for the residence of the Abyssinian princes was a spacious valley in the kingdom of Amhara,[4] surrounded on every side by mountains, of which the summits overhang the middle part. The only passage by which it could be entered was a cavern that passed under a rock, of which it has long been disputed whether it was the

---

[1] Rasselas see Introduction, p. vii
[2] Father of waters Nile
[3] custom see Introduction, p. viii
[4] Amhara see Introduction, p. viii

work of nature or of human industry. The outlet of the cavern was concealed by a thick wood, and the mouth which opened into the valley was closed with gates of iron, forged by the artificers of ancient days, so massy that no man could, without the help of engines, open or shut them.

From the mountains on every side, rivulets descended that filled all the valley with verdure and fertility, and formed a lake in the middle inhabited by fish of every species, and frequented by every fowl whom nature has taught to dip the wing in water. This lake discharged its superfluities by a stream which entered a dark cleft of the mountain on the northern side, and fell with dreadful noise from precipice to precipice till it was heard no more.

The sides of the mountains were covered with trees, the banks of the brooks were diversified with flowers; every blast[5] shook spices from the rocks, and every month dropped fruits upon the ground. All animals that bite the grass or browse the shrub, whether wild or tame, wandered in this extensive circuit, secured from beasts of prey by the mountains which confined them. On one part were flocks and herds feeding in the pastures, on another all the beasts of chase frisking in the lawns; the sprightly kid was bounding on the rocks, the subtle[6] monkey frolicking in the trees, and the solemn elephant reposing in the shade. All the diversities of the world were brought together, the blessings of nature were collected, and its evils extracted and excluded.

The valley, wide and fruitful, supplied its inhabitants with the necessaries of life, and all delights and superfluities were added at the annual visit which the emperor paid his children, when the iron gate was opened to the sound of music; and during eight days every one that resided in the valley was required to propose whatever might contribute to make seclusion pleasant, to fill up the vacancies of attention, and lessen the tediousness of time. Every desire was immediately granted. All the artificers of pleasure were called to gladden the festivity; the musicians exerted the power of harmony, and the

[5] blast "a gust, or puff of wind" (*Dictionary*)
[6] subtle "cunning; artful; sly" (*Dictionary*)

dancers showed their activity before the princes, in hope that they should pass their lives in this blissful captivity, to which these only were admitted whose performance was thought able to add novelty to luxury. Such was the appearance of security and delight which this retirement afforded that they to whom it was new always desired that it might be perpetual; and as those on whom the iron gate had once closed were never suffered to return, the effect of longer experience could not be known. Thus every year produced new schemes of delight and new competitors for imprisonment.

The palace stood on an eminence raised about thirty paces above the surface of the lake. It was divided into many squares or courts, built with greater or less magnificence according to the rank of those for whom they were designed. The roofs were turned into arches of massy stone joined by a cement that grew harder by time, and the building stood from century to century, deriding the solstitial rains and equinoctial hurricanes, without need of reparation.[7]

This house, which was so large as to be fully known to none but some ancient officers who successively inherited the secrets of the place, was built as if suspicion herself had dictated the plan. To every room there was an open and secret passage, every square had a communication with the rest, either from the upper stories by private galleries or by subterranean passages from the lower apartments. Many of the columns had unsuspected cavities, in which a long race of monarchs had reposited their treasures. They then closed up the opening with marble, which was never to be removed but in the utmost exigencies of the kingdom; and recorded their accumulations in a book which was itself concealed in a tower not entered but by the emperor, attended by the prince who stood next in succession.

[7] **reparation** "the act of repairing" (*Dictionary*)

CHAPTER II

THE DISCONTENT OF RASSELAS IN THE HAPPY VALLEY

Here the sons and daughters of Abyssinia lived only to know the soft vicissitudes of pleasure and repose, attended by all that were skilful to delight, and gratified with whatever the senses can enjoy. They wandered in gardens of fragrance, and slept in the fortresses of security. Every art was practised to make them pleased with their own condition. The sages who instructed them told them of nothing but the miseries of public life, and described all beyond the mountains as regions of calamity, where discord was always raging and where man preyed upon man.

To heighten their opinion of their own felicity, they were daily entertained with songs, the subject of which was the *happy valley*. Their appetites were excited by frequent enumerations of different enjoyments, and revelry and merriment was the business of every hour from the dawn of morning to the close of even.

These methods were generally successful; few of the princes had ever wished to enlarge their bounds, but passed their lives in full conviction that they had all within their reach that art or nature could bestow, and pitied those whom fate had excluded from this seat of tranquility, as the sport of chance and the slaves of misery.

Thus they rose in the morning and lay down at night, pleased with each other and with themselves, all but Rasselas, who, in the twenty-sixth year of his age, began to withdraw himself from their pastimes and assemblies, and to delight in solitary walks and silent meditation. He often sat before tables covered with luxury, and forgot to taste the dainties that were placed before him: he rose abruptly in the midst of the song, and hastily retired beyond the sound of music. His attendants observed the change and endeavoured to renew his love of pleasure: he neglected their officiousness,[1] repulsed their invitations,

---

[1] officiousness "forwardness of civility, or respect, or endeavour. Commonly in an ill sense" (*Dictionary*)

and spent day after day on the banks of rivulets sheltered with trees, where he sometimes listened to the birds in the branches, sometimes observed the fish playing in the stream, and anon cast his eyes upon the pastures and mountains filled with animals, of which some were biting the herbage, and some sleeping among the bushes.

This singularity of his humour made him much observed. One of the Sages, in whose conversation he had formerly delighted, followed him secretly in hope of discovering the cause of his disquiet. Rasselas, who knew not that any one was near him, having for some time fixed his eyes upon the goats that were browsing among the rocks, began to compare their condition with his own.

"What," said he, "makes the difference between man and all the rest of the animal creation? Every beast that strays beside me has the same corporal necessities with myself; he is hungry and crops the grass, he is thirsty and drinks the stream, his thirst and hunger are appeased, he is satisfied and sleeps; he rises again and is hungry, he is again fed and is at rest. I am hungry and thirsty like him, but when thirst and hunger cease I am not at rest; I am, like him, pained with want, but am not, like him, satisfied with fulness. The intermediate hours are tedious and gloomy; I long again to be hungry that I may again quicken my attention. The birds peck the berries or the corn, and fly away to the groves where they sit in seeming happiness on the branches, and waste their lives in tuning one unvaried series of sounds. I likewise can call the lutanist and the singer, but the sounds that pleased me yesterday weary me today, and will grow yet more wearisome tomorrow. I can discover within me no power of perception which is not glutted with its proper pleasure, yet I do not feel myself delighted. Man has surely some latent sense for which this place affords no gratification, or he has some desires distinct from sense which must be satisfied before he can be happy."

After this he lifted up his head, and seeing the moon rising, walked towards the palace. As he passed through the fields and saw the animals around him, "Ye," said he, "are happy and need not envy me that walk thus among you, burdened with myself; nor do I, ye gentle beings, envy your felicity; for it is not the felicity of man. I have many distresses from which ye are free; I fear pain when I do not feel it; I sometimes shrink at evils recollected and sometimes start at evils anticipated: surely the equity of providence has balanced peculiar sufferings with peculiar enjoyments."

With observations like these the prince amused himself as he returned, uttering them with a plaintive voice, yet with a look that discovered [2] him to feel some complacence in his own perspicacity, and to receive some solace of the miseries of life from consciousness of the delicacy with which he felt, and the eloquence with which he bewailed them. He mingled cheerfully in the diversions of the evening, and all rejoiced to find that his heart was lightened.

CHAPTER III

The Wants of Him That Wants Nothing

On the next day his old instructor, imagining that he had now made himself acquainted with his disease[1] of mind, was in hope of curing it by counsel, and officiously sought an opportunity of conference, which the prince, having long considered him as one whose intellects[2] were exhausted, was not very willing to afford: "Why," said he, "does this man thus intrude upon me; shall I be never suffered to forget those lectures which pleased only while they were new, and to become new again must be forgotten?" He then walked into the wood and composed himself to his usual meditations; when, before his thoughts had taken any settled form, he perceived his pursuer at his side and was at first prompted by his impatience to go hastily away; but, being unwilling to offend a man whom he had once reverenced and still loved, he invited him to sit down with him on the bank.

The old man, thus encouraged, began to lament the

[2] discovered "to show; to disclose" (*Dictionary*)
[1] disease "morbid state" (*Dictionary*)
[2] intellects intellectual powers

change which had been lately observed in the prince, and to enquire why he so often retired from the pleasures of the palace to loneliness and silence. "I fly from pleasure," said the prince, "because pleasure has ceased to please; I am lonely because I am miserable, and am unwilling to cloud with my presence the happiness of others." "You, Sir," said the sage, "are the first who has complained of misery in the *happy valley*. I hope to convince you that your complaints have no real cause. You are here in full possession of all that the emperor of Abyssinia can bestow; here is neither labour to be endured nor danger to be dreaded, yet here is all that labour or danger can procure or purchase. Look round and tell me which of your wants is without supply: if you want nothing, how are you unhappy?"

"That I want nothing," said the prince, "or that I know not what I want, is the cause of my complaint; if I had any known want, I should have a certain wish; that wish would excite endeavour, and I should not then repine to see the sun move so slowly towards the western mountain, or lament when the day breaks and sleep will no longer hide me from myself. When I see the kids and the lambs chasing one another, I fancy that I should be happy if I had something to pursue. But, possessing all that I can want, I find one day and one hour exactly like another, except that the latter is still more tedious than the former. Let your experience inform me how the day may now seem as short as in my childhood, while nature was yet fresh, and every moment showed me what I never had observed before. I have already enjoyed too much; give me something to desire."

The old man was surprised at this new species of affliction and knew not what to reply, yet was unwilling to be silent. "Sir," said he, "if you had seen the miseries of the world, you would know how to value your present state." "Now," said the prince, "you have given me something to desire; I shall long to see the miseries of the world, since the sight of them is necessary to happiness."

CHAPTER IV

THE PRINCE CONTINUES TO GRIEVE AND MUSE

At this time the sound of music proclaimed the hour of repast, and the conversation was concluded. The old man went away sufficiently discontented to find that his reasonings had produced the only conclusion which they were intended to prevent. But in the decline of life shame and grief are of short duration; whether it be that we bear easily what we have borne long, or that, finding ourselves in age less regarded, we less regard others; or that we look with slight regard upon afflictions to which we know that the hand of death is about to put an end.

The prince, whose views were extended to a wider space, could not speedily quiet his emotions. He had been before terrified at the length of life which nature promised him, because he considered that in a long time much must be endured; he now rejoiced in his youth, because in many years much might be done.

This first beam of hope that had been ever darted into his mind rekindled youth in his cheeks, and doubled the lustre of his eyes. He was fired with the desire of doing something, though he knew not yet with distinctness either end or means.

He was now no longer gloomy and unsocial; but, considering himself as master of a secret stock of happiness, which he could enjoy only by concealing it, he affected to be busy in all schemes of diversion, and endeavoured to make others pleased with the state of which he himself was weary. But pleasures never can be so multiplied or continued as not to leave much of life unemployed; there were many hours, both of the night and day, which he could spend without suspicion in solitary thought. The load of life was much lightened: he went eagerly into the assemblies because he supposed the frequency of his presence necessary to the success of his purposes; he retired gladly to privacy because he had now a subject of thought.

His chief amusement was to picture to himself that world which he had never seen; to place himself in various conditions; to be entangled in imaginary difficulties and to be engaged in wild adventures: but his benevolence always terminated his projects in the relief of distress, the detection of fraud, the defeat of oppression, and the diffusion of happiness.

Thus passed twenty months of the life of Rasselas. He busied himself so intensely in visionary bustle that he forgot his real solitude; and, amidst hourly preparations for the various incidents of human affairs, neglected to consider by what means he should mingle with mankind.

One day, as he was sitting on a bank, he feigned to himself an orphan virgin robbed of her little portion[1] by a treacherous lover, and crying after him for restitution and redress. So strongly was the image impressed upon his mind that he started up in the maid's defence, and run[2] forward to seize the plunderer with all the eagerness of real pursuit. Fear naturally quickens the flight of guilt. Rasselas could not catch the fugitive with his utmost efforts; but, resolving to weary by perseverance him whom he could not surpass in speed, he pressed on till the foot of the mountain stopped his course.

Here he recollected himself and smiled at his own useless impetuosity. Then raising his eyes to the mountain, "This," said he, "is the fatal obstacle that hinders at once the enjoyment of pleasure and the exercise of virtue. How long is it that my hopes and wishes have flown beyond this boundary of my life, which yet I never have attempted to surmount!"

Struck with this reflection, he sat down to muse and remembered that since he first resolved to escape from his confinement, the sun had passed twice over him in his annual course. He now felt a degree of regret with which he had never been before acquainted. He considered how much might have been done in the time which had passed and left nothing real behind it. He compared twenty months with the life of man. "In life," said he, "is not to be counted the ignorance of infancy or imbecility[2] of age. We are long before we are able to think,

[1] portion "part of an inheritance given to a child" (*Dictionary*)
[2] run in the "Grammar" prefixed to Johnson's *Dictionary*, listed as the "preterite" of the verb *to run*.
[3] imbecility "weakness; feebleness of mind or body" (*Dictionary*)

and we soon cease from the power of acting. The true period of human existence may be reasonably estimated as forty years, of which I have mused away the four and twentieth part. What I have lost was certain, for I have certainly possessed it; but of twenty months to come who can assure me?"

The consciousness of his own folly pierced him deeply, and he was long before he could be reconciled to himself. "The rest of my time," said he, "has been lost by the crime or folly of my ancestors and the absurd[3] institutions of my country; I remember it with disgust[4] yet without remorse: but the months that have passed since new light darted into my soul, since I formed a scheme of reasonable felicity, have been squandered by my own fault. I have lost that which can never be restored: I have seen the sun rise and set for twenty months, an idle gazer on the light of heaven: In this time the birds have left the nest of their mother and committed themselves to the woods and to the skies: the kid has forsaken the teat, and learned by degrees to climb the rocks in quest of independent sustenance. I only have made no advances, but am still helpless and ignorant. The moon, by more than twenty changes, admonished me of the flux of life; the stream that rolled before my feet upbraided my inactivity. I sat feasting on intellectual luxury, regardless alike of the examples of the earth, and the instructions of the planets. Twenty months are past, who shall restore them!"

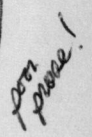

These sorrowful meditations fastened upon his mind; he past four months in resolving to lose no more time in idle resolves, and was awakened to more vigorous exertion by hearing a maid, who had broken a porcelain cup, remark that what cannot be repaired is not to be regretted.

This was obvious; and Rasselas reproached himself that he had not discovered it, having not known, or not considered, how many useful hints are obtained by chance, and how often the mind, hurried by her own ardour to distant views, neglects the truths that lie open before her. He, for a few hours, regretted his regret, and from that

[4] absurd "contrary to reason, used of sentiments or practices" (*Dictionary*)

[5] disgust "ill humor" (*Dictionary*)

time bent his whole mind upon the means of escaping from the valley of happiness.

CHAPTER V

The Prince Meditates His Escape

He now found that it would be very difficult to effect that which it was very easy to suppose effected. When he looked round about him, he saw himself confined by the bars of nature which had never yet been broken, and by the gate, through which none that once had passed it were ever able to return. He was now impatient as an eagle in a grate.[1] He passed week after week in clambering the mountains to see if there was any aperture which the bushes might conceal, but found all the summits inaccessible by their prominence.[2] The iron gate he despaired to open; for it was not only secured with all the power of art, but was always watched by successive sentinels, and was by its position exposed to the perpetual observation of all the inhabitants.

He then examined the cavern through which the waters of the lake were discharged; and, looking down at a time when the sun shone strongly upon its mouth, he discovered it to be full of broken rocks, which, though they permitted the stream to flow through many narrow passages, would stop any body of solid bulk. He returned discouraged and dejected; but, having now known the blessing of hope, resolved never to despair.

In these fruitless searches he spent ten months. The time, however, passed cheerfully away: in the morning he rose with new hope, in the evening applauded his own diligence, and in the night slept sound after his fatigue. He met a thousand amusements which beguiled his labour and diversified his thoughts. He discerned the various instincts of animals and properties of plants, and found

[1] **grate** grated cage
[2] **prominence** protuberance ("Something swelling above the rest" [*Dictionary*])

the place replete with wonders, of which he purposed to solace himself with the contemplation, if he should never be able to accomplish his flight; rejoicing that his endeavours, though yet unsuccessful, had supplied him with a source of inexhaustible enquiry.

But his original curiosity was not yet abated; he resolved to obtain some knowledge of the ways of men. His wish still continued, but his hope grew less. He ceased to survey any longer the walls of his prison, and spared [3] to search by new toils for interstices which he knew could not be found, yet determined to keep his design always in view and lay hold on any expedient that time should offer.

CHAPTER VI

A DISSERTATION ON THE ART OF FLYING[1]

Among the artists that had been allured into the happy valley, to labour for the accommodation and pleasure of its inhabitants, was a man eminent for his knowledge of the mechanic powers, who had contrived many engines[2] both of use and recreation. By a wheel which the stream turned, he forced the water into a tower, whence it was distributed to all the apartments of the palace. He erected a pavilion in the garden, around which he kept the air always cool by artificial showers. One of the groves, appropriated to the ladies, was ventilated by fans, to which the rivulet that run through it gave a constant motion; and instruments of soft music were placed at proper distances, of which some played by the impulse of the wind, and some by the power of the stream.

This artist was sometimes visited by Rasselas, who was pleased with every kind of knowledge, imagining that the

[3] spared "to omit; to forbear" (*Dictionary*)

[1] For much of the material in this chapter, Johnson seems to have drawn on *Mathematical Magick* (1648) by Bishop John Wilkins (1614-72)

[2] engine "any mechanical complication, in which various movements and parts concur to one effect" (*Dictionary*)

time would come when all his acquisitions should be of use to him in the open world. He came one day to amuse himself in his usual manner and found the master busy in building a sailing chariot: he saw that the design was practicable upon a level surface, and with expressions of great esteem solicited its completion. The workman was pleased to find himself so much regarded by the prince, and resolved to gain yet higher honours. "Sir," said he, "you have seen but a small part of what the mechanic sciences can perform. I have been long of opinion that, instead of the tardy conveyance of ships and chariots, man might use the swifter migration[3] of wings; that the fields of air are open to knowledge, and that only ignorance and idleness need crawl upon the ground."

This hint rekindled the prince's desire of passing the mountains; having seen what the mechanist had already performed, he was willing to fancy that he could do more: yet resolved to enquire further before he suffered hope to afflict him by disappointment. "I am afraid," said he to the artist, "that your imagination prevails over your skill, and that you now tell me rather what you wish than what you know. Every animal has his element assigned him; the birds have the air, and man and beasts the earth." "So," replied the mechanist, "fishes have the water, in which yet beasts can swim by nature and men by art. He that can swim needs not despair to fly: to swim is to fly in a grosser fluid, and to fly is to swim in a subtler.[4] We are only to proportion our power of resistance to the different density of the matter through which we are to pass. You will be necessarily upborne by the air if you can renew any impulse upon it faster than the air can recede from the pressure."

"But the exercise of swimming," said the prince, "is very laborious; the strongest limbs are soon wearied; I am afraid the act of flying will be yet more violent, and wings will be of no great use unless we can fly further than we can swim."

"The labour of rising from the ground," said the artist, "will be great, as we see it in the heavier domestic fowls;

[3] migration "act of changing place" (*Dictionary*)
[4] subtler "thin; not dense; not gross" (*Dictionary*)

but, as we mount higher, the earth's attraction and the body's gravity will be gradually diminished, till we shall arrive at a region where the man will float in the air without any tendency to fall: no care will then be necessary but to move forwards, which the gentlest impulse will effect. You, Sir, whose curiosity is so extensive, will easily conceive with what pleasure a philosopher,[5] furnished with wings and hovering in the sky, would see the earth and all its inhabitants rolling beneath him and presenting to him successively, by its diurnal motion, all the countries within the same parallel. How must it amuse the pendent spectator to see the moving scene of land and ocean, cities and deserts! To survey with equal security the marts of trade and the fields of battle; mountains infested by barbarians and fruitful regions gladdened by plenty and lulled by peace! How easily shall we then trace the Nile through all his passage; pass over to distant regions and examine the face of nature from one extremity of the earth to the other!"

"All this," said the prince, "is much to be desired, but I am afraid that no man will be able to breathe in these regions of speculation[6] and tranquility. I have been told that respiration is difficult upon lofty mountains, yet from these precipices, though so high as to produce great tenuity of the air, it is very easy to fall: therefore I suspect that from any height where life can be supported there may be danger of too quick descent."

"Nothing," replied the artist, "will ever be attempted if all possible objections must be first overcome. If you will favour my project I will try the first flight at my own hazard. I have considered the structure of all volant animals and find the folding continuity of the bat's wings mostly easily accommodated to the human form. Upon this model I shall begin my task tomorrow, and in a year expect to tower into the air beyond the malice or pursuit of man. But I will work only on this condition, that the art shall not be divulged and that you shall not require me to make wings for any but ourselves."

[5] philosopher "a man deep in knowledge, either moral or natural" (*Dictionary*)

[6] speculation "examination by the eye; view" (*Dictionary*)

"Why," said Rasselas, "should you envy[7] others so great an advantage? All skill ought to be exerted for universal good; every man has owed much to others and ought to repay the kindness that he has received."

"If men were all virtuous," returned the artist, "I should with great alacrity teach them all to fly. But what would be the security of the good if the bad could at pleasure invade them from the sky? Against an army sailing through the clouds neither walls nor mountains nor seas could afford any security. A flight of northern savages might hover in the wind and light at once with irresistible violence upon the capital of a fruitful region that was rolling under them. Even this valley, the retreat of princes, the abode of happiness, might be violated by the sudden descent of some of the naked nations that swarm on the coast of the southern sea."

The prince promised secrecy and waited for the performance, not wholly hopeless of success. He visited the work from time to time, observed its progress, and remarked many ingenious contrivances to facilitate motion and unite levity with strength. The artist was every day more certain that he should leave vultures and eagles behind him, and the contagion of his confidence seized upon the prince.

In a year the wings were finished, and, on a morning appointed, the maker appeared furnished for flight on a little promontory: he waved his pinions a while to gather air, then leaped from his stand, and in an instant dropped into the lake. His wings, which were of no use in the air, sustained him in the water, and the prince drew him to land, half dead with terror and vexation.

CHAPTER VII

THE PRINCE FINDS A MAN OF LEARNING

The prince was not much afflicted by this disaster, having suffered himself to hope for a happier event only be-

---

[7] envy "to impart unwillingly; to withhold maliciously" (*Dictionary*)

cause he had no other means of escape in view. He still persisted in his design to leave the happy valley by the first opportunity.

His imagination was now at a stand; he had no prospect of entering into the world; and, notwithstanding all his endeavours to support himself, discontent by degrees preyed upon him, and he began again to lose his thoughts in sadness, when the rainy season, which in these countries is periodical, made it inconvenient to wander in the woods.

The rain continued longer and with more violence than had been ever known: the clouds broke on the surrounding mountains and the torrents streamed into the plain on every side, till the cavern was too narrow to discharge the water. The lake overflowed its banks, and all the level of the valley was covered with the inundation. The eminence on which the palace was built and some other spots of rising ground were all that the eye could now discover. The herds and flocks left the pastures, and both the wild beasts and the tame retreated to the mountains.

This inundation confined all the princes to domestic[1] amusements, and the attention of Rasselas was particularly seized by a poem which Imlac rehearsed upon the various conditions of humanity. He commanded the poet to attend him in his apartment and recite his verses a second time; then entering into familiar talk, he thought himself happy in having found a man who knew the world so well and could so skilfully paint the scenes of life. He asked a thousand questions about things to which, though common to all other mortals, his confinement from childhood had kept him a stranger. The poet pitied his ignorance and loved his curiosity, and entertained him from day to day with novelty and instruction, so that the prince regretted the necessity of sleep and longed till the morning should renew his pleasure.

As they were sitting together, the prince commanded Imlac to relate his history and to tell by what accident he was forced, or by what motive induced, to close his life in the happy valley. As he was going to begin his narrative, Rasselas was called to a concert and obliged to restrain his curiosity till the evening.

[1] domestic "private; done at home; not open" (*Dictionary*)

CHAPTER VIII

THE HISTORY OF IMLAC

The close of the day is in the regions of the torrid zone the only season of diversion and entertainment, and it was therefore midnight before the music ceased and the princesses retired. Rasselas then called for his companion and required [1] him to begin the story of his life.

"Sir," said Imlac, "my history will not be long: the life that is devoted to knowledge passes silently away, and is very little diversified by events. To talk in public, to think in solitude, to read and to hear, to inquire, and answer inquiries, is the business of a scholar. He wanders about the world without pomp or terror, and is neither known nor valued but by men like himself.

"I was born in the kingdom of Goiama, at no great distance from the fountain of the Nile. My father was a wealthy merchant, who traded between the inland countries of Africa and the ports of the Red Sea. He was honest, frugal and diligent, but of mean sentiments and narrow comprehension: he desired only to be rich, and to conceal his riches, lest he should be spoiled by the governors of the province."

"Surely," said the prince, "my father must be negligent of his charge if any man in his dominions dares take that which belongs to another. Does he not know that kings are accountable for injustice permitted as well as done? If I were emperor, not the meanest of my subjects should be oppressed with impunity. My blood boils when I am told that a merchant durst not enjoy his honest gains for fear of losing them by the rapacity of power. Name the governor who robbed the people, that I may declare his crimes to the emperor."

"Sir," said Imlac, "your ardour is the natural effect of virtue animated by youth: the time will come when you will acquit your father, and perhaps hear with less impa-

---

[1] required "to demand; to ask a thing as of right" (*Dictionary*)

tience of the governor. Oppression is in the Abyssinian dominions neither frequent nor tolerated; but no form of government has been yet discovered by which cruelty can be wholly prevented. Subordination supposes power on one part and subjection on the other; and if power be in the hands of men, it will sometimes be abused. The vigilance of the supreme magistrate may do much, but much will still remain undone. He can never know all the crimes that are committed, and can seldom punish all that he knows."

"This," said the prince, "I do not understand, but I had rather hear thee than dispute. Continue thy narration."

"My father," proceeded Imlac, "originally intended that I should have no other education than such as might qualify me for commerce; and discovering in me great strength of memory and quickness of apprehension, often declared his hope that I should be some time the richest man in Abyssinia."

"Why," said the prince, "did thy father desire the increase of his wealth when it was already greater than he durst discover or enjoy? I am unwilling to doubt thy veracity, yet inconsistencies cannot both be true."

"Inconsistencies," answered Imlac, "cannot both be right, but, imputed to man, they may both be true. Yet diversity is not inconsistency. My father might expect a time of greater security. However, some desire is necessary to keep life in motion, and he whose real wants are supplied must admit those of fancy."

"This," said the prince, "I can in some measure conceive. I repent that I interrupted thee."

"With this hope," proceeded Imlac, "he sent me to school; but when I had once found the delight of knowledge, and felt the pleasure of intelligence and the pride of invention, I began silently to despise riches and determined to disappoint the purpose of my father, whose grossness of conception raised my pity. I was twenty years old before his tenderness would expose me to the fatigue of travel, in which time I had been instructed by successive masters in all the literature[2] of my native country. As every hour taught me something new, I lived in a continual

---

[2] literature "learning" (*Dictionary*)

course of gratifications; but, as I advanced towards manhood, I lost much of the reverence with which I had been used to look on my instructors; because, when the lesson was ended, I did not find them wiser or better than common men.

"At length my father resolved to initiate me in commerce, and, opening one of his subterranean treasuries, counted out ten thousand pieces of gold. 'This, young man,' said he, 'is the stock with which you must negotiate. I began with less than the fifth part, and you see how diligence and parsimony[3] have increased it. This is your own to waste or to improve. If you squander it by negligence or caprice, you must wait for my death before you will be rich: if in four years you double your stock, we will thenceforward let subordination cease, and live together as friends and partners; for he shall always be equal with me, who is equally skilled in the art of growing rich.'

"We laid our money upon camels, concealed in bales of cheap goods, and travelled to the shore of the Red Sea. When I cast my eye on the expanse of waters my heart bounded like that of a prisoner escaped. I felt an unextinguishable curiosity kindle in my mind, and resolved to snatch this opportunity of seeing the manners of other nations and of learning sciences unknown in Abyssinia.

"I remembered that my father had obliged me to the improvement of my stock, not by a promise which I ought not to violate, but by a penalty which I was at liberty to incur, and therefore determined to gratify my predominant desire, and by drinking at the fountains of knowledge to quench the thirst of curiosity.

"As I was supposed to trade without connection with my father, it was easy for me to become acquainted with the master of a ship, and procure a passage to some other country. I had no motives of choice to regulate my voyage; it was sufficient for me that, wherever I wandered, I should see a country which I had not seen before. I therefore entered a ship bound for Surat,[4] having left a letter for my father declaring my intention."

[3] parsimony "frugality" (*Dictionary*)
[4] Surat port city of India

CHAPTER IX

THE HISTORY OF IMLAC CONTINUED

"When I first entered upon the world of waters and lost sight of land, I looked round about me with pleasing terror, and thinking my soul enlarged by the boundless prospect, imagined that I could gaze round for ever without satiety; but in a short time I grew weary of looking on barren uniformity, where I could only see again what I had already seen. I then descended into the ship, and doubted for a while whether all my future pleasures would not end like this in disgust and disappointment. Yet, surely, said I, the ocean and the land are very different; the only variety of water is rest and motion, but the earth has mountains and valleys, deserts and cities: it is inhabited by men of different customs and contrary opinions; and I may hope to find variety in life though I should miss it in nature.

"With this thought I quieted my mind, and amused myself during the voyage; sometimes by learning from the sailors the art of navigation, which I have never practised, and sometimes by forming schemes for my conduct in different situations, in not one of which I have been ever placed.

"I was almost weary of my naval [1] amusements when we landed safely at Surat. I secured my money, and purchasing some commodities for show, joined myself to a caravan that was passing into the inland country.[2] My companions, for some reason or other, conjecturing that I was rich and, by my inquiries and admiration,[3] finding that I was ignorant, considered me as a novice whom they had a right to cheat, and who was to learn at the usual expense the

[1] naval "consisting of" or "belonging to ships" (*Dictionary*)
[2] In journeying from Surat inland toward Agra, Imlac traversed a route often followed by early travelers and trade caravans.
[3] admiration "wonder" (*Dictionary*)

art of fraud. They exposed me to the theft of servants and the exaction of officers, and saw me plundered upon false pretences, without any advantage to themselves but that of rejoicing in the superiority of their own knowledge."

"Stop a moment," said the prince. "Is there such depravity in man as that he should injure another without benefit to himself? I can easily conceive that all are pleased with superiority; but your ignorance was merely accidental, which, being neither your crime nor your folly, could afford them no reason to applaud themselves; and the knowledge which they had and which you wanted they might as effectually have shown by warning, as betraying you."

"Pride," said Imlac, "is seldom delicate, it will please itself with very mean advantages; and envy feels not its own happiness but when it may be compared with the misery of others. They were my enemies because they grieved to think me rich, and my oppressors because they delighted to find me weak."

"Proceed," said the prince: "I doubt not of the facts which you relate, but imagine that you impute them to mistaken motives."

"In this company," said Imlac, "I arrived at Agra, the capital of Indostan, the city in which the great Mogul commonly resides. I applied myself to the language of the country, and in a few months was able to converse with the learned men; some of whom I found morose and reserved, and others easy and communicative; some were unwilling to teach another what they had with difficulty learned themselves; and some showed that the end of their studies was to gain the dignity of instructing.

"To the tutor of the young princes I recommended myself so much that I was presented to the emperor as a man of uncommon knowledge. The emperor asked me many questions concerning my country and my travels; and though I cannot now recollect any thing that he uttered above the power of a common man, he dismissed me astonished at his wisdom and enamoured of his goodness.

"My credit was now so high that the merchants with whom I had travelled applied to me for recommendations to the ladies of the court. I was surprised at their confidence of solicitation and gently reproached them with their practices on the road. They heard me with cold indifference and showed no tokens of shame or sorrow.

"They then urged their request with the offer of a bribe; but what I would not do for kindness I would not do for money; and refused them, not because they had injured me, but because I would not enable them to injure others; for I knew they would have made use of my credit to cheat those who should buy their wares.

"Having resided at Agra till there was no more to be learned, I travelled into Persia, where I saw many remains of ancient magnificence and observed many new accommodations[4] of life. The Persians are a nation eminently social, and their assemblies afforded me daily opportunities of remarking characters and manners, and of tracing human nature through all its variations.

"From Persia I passed into Arabia, where I saw a nation at once pastoral and warlike; who live without any settled habitation; whose only wealth is their flocks and herds; and who have yet carried on, through all ages, an hereditary war with all mankind, though they neither covet nor envy their possessions."

CHAPTER X

IMLAC'S HISTORY CONTINUED.
A DISSERTATION UPON POETRY[1]

"Wherever I went, I found that Poetry was considered as the highest learning, and regarded with a veneration somewhat approaching to that which man would pay to the Angelic Nature. And it yet fills me with wonder that, in almost all countries, the most ancient poets are considered as the best; whether it be that every other kind of knowledge is an acquisition gradually attained, and poetry

---

[4] accommodations "conveniences, things requisite to ease or refreshment" (*Dictionary*)

[1] Imlac's dissertation on poetry, one of the most famous chapters in *Rasselas*, contains many pronouncements on poetry and poets which were also expressed by earlier English critics.

is a gift conferred at once; or that the first poetry of every nation surprised them as a novelty, and retained the credit by consent which it received by accident at first; or whether, as the province of poetry is to describe Nature and Passion, which are always the same, the first writers took possession of the most striking objects for description and the most probable occurrences for fiction, and left nothing to those that followed them but transcription of the same events and new combinations of the same images. Whatever be the reason, it is commonly observed that the early writers are in possession of nature, and their followers of art: that the first excel in strength and invention, and the latter in elegance and refinement.

"I was desirous to add my name to this illustrious fraternity. I read all the poets of Persia and Arabia and was able to repeat by memory the volumes[2] that are suspended in the mosque of Mecca. But I soon found that no man was ever great by imitation. My desire of excellence impelled me to transfer my attention to nature and to life. Nature was to be my subject, and men to be my auditors: I could never describe what I had not seen: I could not hope to move those with delight or terror whose interests and opinions I did not understand.

"Being now resolved to be a poet, I saw everything with a new purpose; my sphere of attention was suddenly magnified: no kind of knowledge was to be overlooked. I ranged mountains and deserts for images and resemblances, and pictured upon my mind every tree of the forest and flower of the valley. I observed with equal care the crags of the rock and the pinnacles of the palace. Sometimes I wandered along the mazes of the rivulet, and sometimes watched the changes of the summer clouds. To a poet nothing can be useless. Whatever is beautiful, and whatever is dreadful, must be familiar to his imagination: he must be conversant with all that is awfully vast or elegantly little. The plants of the garden, the animals of the wood, the minerals of the earth, and meteors of the sky must all concur to store his mind with inexhaustible variety: for every idea is useful for the enforcement or decoration of moral or religious truth; and he who knows

[2] **volumes** works which received prizes at "fairs of poetry" held annually, according to tradition, in Arabia

most will have most power of diversifying his scenes, and of gratifying his reader with remote allusions and unexpected instruction.

"All the appearances of nature I was therefore careful to study, and every country which I have surveyed has contributed something to my poetical powers."

"In so wide a survey," said the prince, "you must surely have left much unobserved. I have lived till now within the circuit of these mountains, and yet cannot walk abroad without the sight of something which I had never beheld before or never heeded."

"The business of a poet," said Imlac, "is to examine, not the individual, but the species; to remark general properties and large appearances: he does not number the streaks of the tulip or describe the different shades in the verdure of the forest. He is to exhibit in his portraits of nature such prominent and striking features as recall the original to every mind; and must neglect the minuter discriminations, which one may have remarked and another have neglected, for those characteristics which are alike obvious to vigilance and carelessness.

"But the knowledge of nature is only half the task of a poet; he must be acquainted likewise with all the modes of life. His character requires that he estimate the happiness and misery of every condition; observe the power of all the passions in all their combinations, and trace the changes of the human mind as they are modified by various institutions and accidental influences of climate or custom, from the sprightliness of infancy to the despondence of decrepitude. He must divest himself of the prejudices of his age or country; he must consider right and wrong in their abstracted [3] and invariable state; he must disregard present laws and opinions and rise to general and transcendental truths, which will always be the same: he must therefore content himself with the slow progress of his name; contemn the applause of his own time, and commit his claims to the justice of posterity. He must write as the interpreter of nature and the legislator of mankind, and consider himself as presiding over the thoughts and manners of future generations; as a being superior to time and place.

[3] abstracted "refined, abstruse" (*Dictionary*)

"His labour is not yet at an end: he must know many languages and many sciences; and, that his style may be worthy of his thoughts, must, by incessant practice, familiarize to himself every delicacy of speech and grace of harmony."

CHAPTER XI

IMLAC'S NARRATIVE CONTINUED. A HINT ON PILGRIMAGE

Imlac now felt the enthusiastic[1] fit and was proceeding to aggrandize his own profession when the prince cried out, "Enough! Thou hast convinced me that no human being can ever be a poet. Proceed with thy narration."

"To be a poet," said Imlac, "is indeed very difficult."

"So difficult," returned the prince, "that I will at present hear no more of his labours. Tell me whither you went when you had seen Persia."

"From Persia," said the poet, "I travelled through Syria and for three years resided in Palestine, where I conversed with great numbers of the northern and western nations of Europe; the nations which are now in possession of all power and all knowledge; whose armies are irresistible and whose fleets command the remotest parts of the globe. When I compared these men with the natives of our own kingdom and those that surround us, they appeared almost another order of beings. In their countries it is difficult to wish for any thing that may not be obtained: a thousand arts of which we never heard are continually labouring for their convenience and pleasure; and whatever their own climate has denied them is supplied by their commerce."

"By what means," said the prince, "are the Europeans thus powerful? or why, since they can so easily visit Asia and Africa for trade or conquest, cannot the Asiatics and Africans invade their coasts, plant colonies in their ports, and give laws to their natural princes? The same wind that carries them back would bring us thither."

[1] enthusiastic "elevated in fancy; exalted in ideas" (*Dictionary*)

"They are more powerful, Sir, than we," answered Imlac, "because they are wiser; knowledge will always predominate over ignorance, as man governs the other animals. But why their knowledge is more than ours, I know not what reason can be given but the unsearchable will of the Supreme Being."

"When," said the prince with a sigh, "shall I be able to visit Palestine and mingle with this mighty confluence of nations? Till that happy moment shall arrive, let me fill up the time with such representations as thou canst give me. I am not ignorant of the motive that assembles such numbers in that place, and cannot but consider it as the center of wisdom and piety, to which the best and wisest men of every land must be continually resorting."

"There are some nations," said Imlac, "that send few visitants to Palestine; for many numerous and learned sects in Europe concur to censure pilgrimage as superstitious or deride it as ridiculous."

"You know," said the prince, "how little my life has made me acquainted with diversity of opinions: it will be too long to hear the arguments on both sides; you, that have considered them, tell me the result."

"Pilgrimage," said Imlac, "like many other acts of piety, may be reasonable or superstitious according to the principles upon which it is performed. Long journeys in search of truth are not commanded. Truth such as is necessary to the regulation of life is always found where it is honestly sought. Change of place is no natural cause of the increase of piety, for it inevitably produces dissipation of mind. Yet, since men go every day to view the fields where great actions have been performed, and return with stronger impressions of the event, curiosity of the same kind may naturally dispose us to view that country whence our religion had its beginning; and I believe no man surveys those awful scenes without some confirmation of holy resolutions. That the Supreme Being may be more easily propitiated in one place than in another is the dream of idle superstition; but that some places may operate upon our own minds in an uncommon manner is an opinion which hourly experience will justify. He who supposes that his vices may be more successfully combated in Palestine will, perhaps, find himself mistaken, yet he may go thither without folly: he who thinks they will be more freely pardoned, dishonours at once his reason and religion."

"These," said the prince, "are European distinctions. I will consider them another time. What have you found to be the effect of knowledge? Are those nations happier than we?"

"There is so much infelicity," said the poet, "in the world that scarce any man has leisure from his own distresses to estimate the comparative happiness of others. Knowledge is certainly one of the means of pleasure, as is confessed by the natural desire which every mind feels of increasing its ideas. Ignorance is mere privation, by which nothing can be produced: it is a vacuity in which the soul sits motionless and torpid for want of attraction; and, without knowing why, we always rejoice when we learn and grieve when we forget. I am therefore inclined to conclude that, if nothing counteracts the natural consequence of learning, we grow more happy as our minds take a wider range.

"In enumerating the particular comforts of life we shall find many advantages on the side of the Europeans. They cure wounds and diseases with which we languish and perish. We suffer inclemencies of weather which they can obviate. They have engines for the despatch of many laborious works which we must perform by manual industry. There is such communication between distant places that one friend can hardly be said to be absent from another. Their policy[2] removes all public inconveniences: they have roads cut through their mountains and bridges laid upon their rivers. And, if we descend to the privacies of life, their habitations are more commodious and their possessions are more secure."

"They are surely happy," said the prince, "who have all these conveniences, of which I envy none so much as the facility with which separated friends interchange their thoughts."

"The Europeans," answered Imlac, "are less unhappy than we, but they are not happy. Human life is everywhere a state in which much is to be endured, and little to be enjoyed."

[2] policy "art of government" (*Dictionary*)

CHAPTER XII

The Story of Imlac Continued

"I am not yet willing," said the prince, "to suppose that happiness is so parsimoniously distributed to mortals; nor can believe but that, if I had the choice of life, I should be able to fill every day with pleasure. I would injure no man and should provoke no resentment: I would relieve every distress and should enjoy the benedictions of gratitude. I would choose my friends among the wise and my wife among the virtuous; and therefore should be in no danger from treachery or unkindness. My children should, by my care, be learned and pious, and would repay to my age what their childhood had received. What would dare to molest him who might call on every side to thousands enriched by his bounty or assisted by his power? And why should not life glide quietly away in the soft reciprocation of protection and reverence? All this may be done without the help of European refinements, which appear by their effects to be rather specious than useful. Let us leave them and pursue our journey."

"From Palestine," said Imlac, "I passed through many regions of Asia; in the more civilized kingdoms as a trader, and among the Barbarians of the mountains as a pilgrim. At last I began to long for my native country, that I might repose after my travels and fatigues in the places where I had spent my earliest years, and gladden my old companions with the recital of my adventures. Often did I figure[1] to myself those with whom I had sported away the gay hours of dawning life sitting round me in its evening, wondering at my tales and listening to my counsels.

"When this thought had taken possession of my mind, I considered every moment as wasted which did not bring me nearer to Abyssinia. I hastened into Egypt, and, notwithstanding my impatience, was detained ten months

[1] figure "to image in the mind" (*Dictionary*)

in the contemplation of its ancient magnificence and in enquiries after the remains of its ancient learning. I found in Cairo a mixture of all nations; some brought thither by the love of knowledge, some by the hope of gain, and many by the desire of living after their own manner without observation, and of lying hid in the obscurity of multitudes: for in a city populous as Cairo it is possible to obtain at the same time the gratifications of society and the secrecy of solitude.

"From Cairo I travelled to Suez and embarked on the Red Sea, passing along the coast till I arrived at the port from which I had departed twenty years before. Here I joined myself to a caravan and re-entered my native country.

"I now expected the caresses of my kinsmen and the congratulations of my friends, and was not without hope that my father, whatever value he had set upon riches, would own with gladness and pride a son who was able to add to the felicity and honour of the nation. But I was soon convinced that my thoughts were vain. My father had been dead fourteen years, having divided his wealth among my brothers, who were removed to some other provinces. Of my companions the greater part was in the grave, of the rest some could with difficulty remember me, and some considered me as one corrupted by foreign manners.

"A man used to vicissitudes is not easily dejected. I forgot, after a time, my disappointment, and endeavoured to recommend myself to the nobles of the kingdom: they admitted me to their tables, heard my story, and dismissed me. I opened a school, and was prohibited to teach. I then resolved to sit down in the quiet of domestic life, and addressed a lady that was fond of my conversation but rejected my suit because my father was a merchant.

"Wearied at last with solicitation and repulses, I resolved to hide myself forever from the world and depend no longer on the opinion or caprice of others. I waited for the time when the gate of the *happy valley* should open, that I might bid farewell to hope and fear: the day came; my performance was distinguished with favour, and I resigned myself with joy to perpetual confinement."

"Hast thou here found happiness at last?" said Rasselas.

"Tell me without reserve; art thou content with thy condition? or dost thou wish to be again wandering and inquiring? All the inhabitants of this valley celebrate their lot and, at the annual visit of the emperor, invite others to partake of their felicity."

"Great prince," said Imlac, "I shall speak the truth: I know not one of all your attendants who does not lament the hour when he entered this retreat. I am less unhappy than the rest because I have a mind replete with images which I can vary and combine at pleasure. I can amuse my solitude by the renovation of the knowledge which begins to fade from my memory, and by recollection of the accidents of my past life. Yet all this ends in the sorrowful consideration that my acquirements are now useless and that none of my pleasures can be again enjoyed. The rest, whose minds have no impression but of the present moment, are either corroded by malignant passions or sit stupid in the gloom of perpetual vacancy." [2]

"What passions can infest those," said the prince, "who have no rivals? We are in a place where impotence precludes malice, and where all envy is repressed by community of enjoyments."

"There may be community," said Imlac, "of material possessions, but there can never be community of love or of esteem. It must happen that one will please more than another; he that knows himself despised will always be envious; and still more envious and malevolent, if he is condemned to live in the presence of those who despise him. The invitations by which they allure others to a state which they feel to be wretched, proceed from the natural malignity of hopeless misery. They are weary of themselves and of each other, and expect to find relief in new companions. They envy the liberty which their folly has forfeited and would gladly see all mankind imprisoned like themselves.

"From this crime, however, I am wholly free. No man can say that he is wretched by my persuasion. I look with pity on the crowds who are annually soliciting admission to captivity, and wish that it were lawful for me to warn them of their danger."

"My dear Imlac," said the prince, "I will open to thee

[2] **vacancy** "listlessness; emptiness of thought" (*Dictionary*)

my whole heart. I have long meditated an escape from the happy valley. I have examined the mountains on every side, but find myself insuperably barred: teach me the way to break my prison; thou shalt be the companion of my flight, the guide of my rambles, the partner of my fortune, and my sole director in the *choice of life*."

"Sir," answered the poet, "your escape will be difficult and, perhaps, you may soon repent your curiosity. The world, which you figure to yourself smooth and quiet as the lake in the valley, you will find a sea foaming with tempests and boiling with whirlpools: you will be sometimes overwhelmed by the waves of violence and sometimes dashed against the rocks of treachery. Amidst wrongs and frauds, competitions and anxieties, you will wish a thousand times for these seats of quiet, and willingly quit hope to be free from fear."

"Do not seek to deter me from my purpose," said the prince: "I am impatient to see what thou hast seen; and, since thou art thyself weary of the valley, it is evident that thy former state was better than this. Whatever be the consequence of my experiment, I am resolved to judge with my own eyes of the various conditions of men and then to make deliberately my *choice of life*."

"I am afraid," said Imlac, "you are hindered by stronger restraints than my persuasions; yet, if your determination is fixed, I do not counsel you to despair. Few things are impossible to diligence and skill."

CHAPTER XIII

Rasselas Discovers the Means of Escape

The prince now dismissed his favourite to rest, but the narrative of wonders and novelties filled his mind with perturbation. He revolved [1] all that he had heard and prepared innumerable questions for the morning.

Much of his uneasiness was now removed. He had a friend to whom he could impart his thoughts, and whose experience could assist him in his designs. His heart was

---

[1] **revolved** "to consider; to meditate on" (*Dictionary*)

no longer condemned to swell with silent vexation. He thought that even the *happy valley* might be endured with such a companion, and that, if they could range the world together, he should have nothing further to desire.

In a few days the water was discharged and the ground dried. The prince and Imlac then walked out together to converse without the notice of the rest. The prince, whose thoughts were always on the wing, as he passed by the gate, said, with a countenance of sorrow, "Why art thou so strong, and why is man so weak?"

"Man is not weak," answered his companion; "knowledge is more than equivalent to force. The master of mechanics laughs at strength. I can burst the gate but cannot do it secretly. Some other expedient must be tried."

As they were walking on the side of the mountain, they observed that the conies,[2] which the rain had driven from their burrows, had taken shelter among the bushes and formed holes behind them, tending upwards in an oblique line. "It has been the opinion of antiquity," said Imlac, "that human reason borrowed many arts from the instinct of animals; let us, therefore, not think ourselves degraded by learning from the coney. We may escape by piercing the mountain in the same direction. We will begin where the summit hangs over the middle part, and labour upward till we shall issue out beyond the prominence."

The eyes of the prince, when he heard this proposal, sparkled with joy. The execution was easy, and the success certain.

No time was now lost. They hastened early in the morning to choose a place proper for their mine. They clambered with great fatigue among crags and brambles, and returned without having discovered any part that favoured their design. The second and the third day were spent in the same manner and with the same frustration. But, on the fourth, they found a small cavern concealed by a thicket, where they resolved to make their experiment.

Imlac procured instruments proper to hew stone and remove earth, and they fell to their work on the next day with more eagerness than vigour. They were presently exhausted by their efforts, and sat down to pant upon the

[2] conies rabbits

grass. The prince, for a moment, appeared to be discouraged. "Sir," said his companion, "practice will enable us to continue our labour for a longer time; mark, however, how far we have advanced, and you will find that our toil will some time have an end. Great works are performed, not by strength, but perseverance: yonder palace was raised by single stones, yet you see its height and spaciousness. He that shall walk with vigour three hours a day will pass in seven years a space equal to the circumference of the globe."

They returned to their work day after day, and, in a short time, found a fissure in the rock which enabled them to pass far with very little obstruction. This Rasselas considered as a good omen. "Do not disturb your mind," said Imlac, "with other hopes or fears than reason may suggest: if you are pleased with prognostics of good, you will be terrified likewise with tokens of evil, and your whole life will be a prey to superstition. Whatever facilitates our work is more than an omen, it is a cause of success. This is one of those pleasing surprises which often happen to active resolution. Many things difficult to design prove easy to performance."

CHAPTER XIV

RASSELAS AND IMLAC RECEIVE AN UNEXPECTED VISIT

They had now wrought their way to the middle, and solaced their toil with the approach of liberty, when the prince, coming down to refresh himself with air, found his sister Nekayah standing before the mouth of the cavity. He started and stood confused, afraid to tell his design and yet hopeless to conceal it. A few moments determined him to repose on her fidelity and secure her secrecy by a declaration without reserve.

"Do not imagine," said the princess, "that I came hither as a spy: I had long observed from my window that you and Imlac directed your walk every day towards the same point, but I did not suppose you had any better reason for the preference than a cooler shade or more fragrant bank; nor followed you with any other design than to partake of your conversation. Since then not suspicion but fondness has detected you, let me not lose the advantage of my discovery. I am equally weary of confinement with yourself and not less desirous of knowing what is done or suffered in the world. Permit me to fly with you from this tasteless tranquility, which will yet grow more loathsome when you have left me. You may deny me to accompany you, but cannot hinder me from following."

The prince, who loved Nekayah above his other sisters, had no inclination to refuse her request, and grieved that he had lost an opportunity of showing his confidence by a voluntary communication. It was therefore agreed that she should leave the valley with them; and that, in the mean time, she should watch lest any other straggler[1] should, by chance or curiosity, follow them to the mountain.

At length their labour was at an end; they saw light beyond the prominence, and, issuing to the top of the mountain, beheld the Nile, yet a narrow current, wandering beneath them.

The prince looked round with rapture, anticipated all the pleasures of travel, and in thought was already transported beyond his father's dominions. Imlac, though very joyful at his escape, had less expectation of pleasure in the world, which he had before tried and of which he had been weary.

Rasselas was so much delighted with a wider horizon that he could not soon be persuaded to return into the valley. He informed his sister that the way was open, and that nothing now remained but to prepare for their departure.

CHAPTER XV

THE PRINCE AND PRINCESS LEAVE THE VALLEY AND SEE MANY WONDERS

The prince and princess had jewels sufficient to make them rich whenever they came into a place of commerce,

[1] straggler "a wanderer; a rover" (*Dictionary*)

which, by Imlac's direction, they hid in their clothes, and, on the night of the next full moon, all left the valley. The princess was followed only by a single favourite, who did not know whither she was going.

They clambered through the cavity and began to go down on the other side. The princess and her maid turned their eyes towards every part and, seeing nothing to bound their prospect, considered themselves as in danger of being lost in a dreary vacuity. They stopped and trembled. "I am almost afraid," said the princess, "to begin a journey of which I cannot perceive an end, and to venture into this immense plain where I may be approached on every side by men whom I never saw." The prince felt nearly the same emotions, though he thought it more manly to conceal them.

Imlac smiled at their terrors, and encouraged them to proceed; but the princess continued irresolute till she had been imperceptibly drawn forward too far to return.

In the morning they found some shepherds in the field, who set milk and fruits before them. The princess wondered that she did not see a palace ready for her reception, and a table spread with delicacies; but, being faint and hungry, she drank the milk and eat[1] the fruits, and thought them of a higher flavour than the products of the valley.

They travelled forward by easy journeys,[2] being all unaccustomed to toil or difficulty, and knowing that though they might be missed they could not be pursued. In a few days they came into a more populous region, where Imlac was diverted with the admiration which his companions expressed at the diversity of manners, stations and employments.

Their dress was such as might not bring upon them the suspicion of having any thing to conceal, yet the prince, wherever he came, expected to be obeyed, and the princess was frightened because those that came into her presence did not prostrate themselves before her. Imlac was forced to observe them with great vigilance, lest they should betray their rank by their unusual behaviour, and

[1] eat according to Johnson's *Dictionary*, the "preterite" of the verb *to eat* is either "ate" or "eat"

[2] journeys "the travel of a day" (*Dictionary*)

detained them several weeks in the first village to accustom them to the sight of common mortals.

By degrees the royal wanderers were taught to understand that they had for a time laid aside their dignity, and were to expect only such regard as liberality and courtesy could procure. And Imlac, having by many admonitions prepared them to endure the tumults of a port and the ruggedness[3] of the commercial race, brought them down to the sea-coast.

The prince and his sister, to whom everything was new, were gratified equally at all places, and therefore remained for some months at the port without any inclination to pass further. Imlac was content with their stay because he did not think it safe to expose them, unpractised in the world, to the hazards of a foreign country.

At last he began to fear lest they should be discovered, and proposed to fix a day for their departure. They had no pretensions[4] to judge for themselves and referred the whole scheme to his direction. He therefore took passage in a ship to Suez; and, when the time came, with great difficulty prevailed on the princess to enter the vessel. They had a quick and prosperous voyage, and from Suez travelled by land to Cairo.

CHAPTER XVI

They Enter Cairo and Find Every Man Happy

As they approached the city, which filled the strangers with astonishment, "This," said Imlac to the prince, "is the place where travellers and merchants assemble from all the corners of the earth. You will here find men of every character and every occupation. Commerce is here honourable: I will act as a merchant, and you shall live as strangers, who have no other end of travel than curiosity; it will soon be observed that we are rich; our reputation will procure us access to all whom we shall desire

[3] ruggedness "roughness, asperity" (*Dictionary*)
[4] pretensions "claim true or false" (*Dictionary*)

to know; you will see all the conditions of humanity and enable yourself at leisure to make your *choice of life*."

They now entered the town, stunned by the noise and offended by the crowds. Instruction had not yet so prevailed over habit but that they wondered to see themselves pass undistinguished along the street, and met by the lowest of the people without reverence or notice. The princess could not at first bear the thought of being levelled with the vulgar, and for some days continued in her chamber, where she was served by her favourite Pekuah as in the palace of the valley.

Imlac, who understood traffic,[1] sold part of the jewels the next day and hired a house, which he adorned with such magnificence that he was immediately considered as a merchant of great wealth. His politeness attracted many acquaintance,[2] and his generosity made him courted by many dependents. His table was crowded by men of every nation, who all admired his knowledge and solicited his favour. His companions, not being able to mix in the conversation, could make no discovery of their ignorance or surprise, and were gradually initiated in the world as they gained knowledge of the language.

The prince had, by frequent lectures, been taught the use and nature of money; but the ladies could not, for a long time, comprehend what the merchants did with small pieces of gold and silver, or why things of so little use should be received as equivalent to the necessaries of life.

They studied the language two years, while Imlac was preparing to set before them the various ranks and conditions of mankind. He grew acquainted with all who had anything uncommon in their fortune or conduct. He frequented the voluptuous[3] and the frugal, the idle and the busy, the merchants and the men of learning.

The prince, being now able to converse with fluency, and having learned the caution necessary to be observed in his intercourse with strangers, began to accompany

[1] traffic "commerce" (*Dictionary*)

[2] acquaintance "in this sense, the plural is, in some authors, *acquaintance*, in others, *acquaintances*" (*Dictionary*)

[3] voluptuous "given to excess of pleasure; luxurious" (*Dictionary*)

Imlac to places of resort, and to enter into all assemblies that he might make his *choice of life*.

For some time he thought choice needless because all appeared to him equally happy. Wherever he went he met gaiety and kindness, and heard the song of joy or the laugh of carelessness. He began to believe that the world overflowed with universal plenty, and that nothing was withheld either from want or merit; that every hand showered liberality and every heart melted with benevolence: "and who then," says he, "will be suffered to be wretched?"

Imlac permitted the pleasing delusion and was unwilling to crush the hope of inexperience, till one day, having sat a while silent, "I know not," said the prince, "what can be the reason that I am more unhappy than any of our friends. I see them perpetually and unalterably cheerful, but feel my own mind restless and uneasy. I am unsatisfied with those pleasures which I seem most to court; I live in the crowds of jollity not so much to enjoy company as to shun myself, and am only loud and merry to conceal my sadness."

"Every man," said Imlac, "may, by examining his own mind, guess what passes in the minds of others: when you feel that your own gaiety is counterfeit, it may justly lead you to suspect that of your companions not to be sincere. Envy is commonly reciprocal. We are long before we are convinced that happiness is never to be found, and each believes it possessed by others, to keep alive the hope of obtaining it for himself. In the assembly where you passed the last night, there appeared such sprightliness of air and volatility of fancy as might have suited beings of an higher order, formed to inhabit serener regions inaccessible to care or sorrow: yet, believe me, prince, there was not one who did not dread the moment when solitude should deliver him to the tyranny of reflection."

"This," said the prince, "may be true of others, since it is true of me; yet, whatever be the general infelicity of man, one condition is more happy than another, and wisdom surely directs us to take the least evil in the *choice of life*."

"The causes of good and evil," answered Imlac, "are so various and uncertain, so often entangled with each other, so diversified by various relations, and so much subject to accidents which cannot be foreseen, that he who would fix his condition upon incontestable reasons of preference must live and die enquiring and deliberating."

"But surely," said Rasselas, "the wise men, to whom we listen with reverence and wonder, chose that mode of life for themselves which they thought most likely to make them happy."

"Very few," said the poet, "live by choice. Every man is placed in his present condition by causes which acted without his foresight, and with which he did not always willingly co-operate; and therefore you will rarely meet one who does not think the lot of his neighbour better than his own."

"I am pleased to think," said the prince, "that my birth has given me at least one advantage over others, by enabling me to determine for myself. I have here the world before me; I will review it at leisure: surely happiness is somewhere to be found."

CHAPTER XVII

THE PRINCE ASSOCIATES WITH YOUNG MEN
OF SPIRIT AND GAIETY

Rasselas rose next day and resolved to begin his experiments upon life. "Youth," cried he, "is the time of gladness: I will join myself to the young men whose only business is to gratify their desires and whose time is all spent in a succession of enjoyments."

To such societies he was readily admitted, but a few days brought him back weary and disgusted. Their mirth was without images,[1] their laughter without motive; their pleasures were gross and sensual, in which the mind had no part; their conduct was at once wild and mean; they laughed at order and at law, but the frown of power dejected, and the eye of wisdom abashed them.

The prince soon concluded that he should never be happy in a course of life of which he was ashamed. He thought it unsuitable to a reasonable being to act without

[1] images ideas

a plan, and to be sad or cheerful only by chance. "Happiness," said he, "must be something solid and permanent, without fear and without uncertainty."

But his young companions had gained so much of his regard by their frankness and courtesy that he could not leave them without warning and remonstrance. "My friends," said he, "I have seriously considered our manners and our prospects, and find that we have mistaken our own interest. The first years of man must make provision for the last. He that never thinks never can be wise. Perpetual levity must end in ignorance; and intemperance, though it may fire the spirits for an hour, will make life short or miserable. Let us consider that youth is of no long duration and that in maturer age, when the enchantments of fancy shall cease and phantoms of delight dance no more about us, we shall have no comforts but the esteem of wise men and the means of doing good. Let us, therefore, stop, while to stop is in our power: let us live as men who are sometime to grow old, and to whom it will be the most dreadful of all evils not to count their past years but by follies, and to be reminded of their former luxuriance of health only by the maladies which riot has produced."

They stared a while in silence one upon another and, at last, drove him away by a general chorus of continued laughter.

The consciousness that his sentiments were just, and his intentions kind, was scarcely sufficient to support him against the horror of derision. But he recovered his tranquility and pursued his search.

CHAPTER XVIII

The Prince Finds a Wise and Happy Man

As he was one day walking in the street, he saw a spacious building which all were, by the open doors, invited to enter: he followed the stream of people and found it a hall or school of declamation, in which professors read lectures to their auditory. He fixed his eye upon a sage raised above the rest, who discoursed with great energy on the government of the passions.[1] His look was venerable, his action graceful, his pronunciation clear, and his diction elegant. He showed, with great strength of sentiment and variety of illustration, that human nature is degraded and debased when the lower faculties predominate over the higher; that when fancy, the parent of passion, usurps the dominion of the mind, nothing ensues but the natural effect of unlawful government, perturbation and confusion; that she betrays the fortresses of the intellect to rebels, and excites her children to sedition against reason their lawful sovereign. He compared reason to the sun, of which the light is constant, uniform, and lasting; and fancy to a meteor, of bright but transitory lustre, irregular in its motion and delusive in its direction.

He then communicated the various precepts given from time to time for the conquest of passion, and displayed the happiness of those who had obtained the important victory, after which man is no longer the slave of fear nor the fool of hope; is no more emaciated by envy, inflamed by anger, emasculated by tenderness, or depressed by grief; but walks on calmly through the tumults or the privacies of life, as the sun pursues alike his course through the calm or the stormy sky.

He enumerated many examples of heroes immovable by pain or pleasure, who looked with indifference on those modes or accidents to which the vulgar give the names of good or evil. He exhorted his hearers to lay aside their prejudices, and arm themselves against the shafts of malice or misfortune by invulnerable patience; concluding that this state only was happiness and that this happiness was in everyone's power.

Rasselas listened to him with the veneration due to the instructions of a superior being, and, waiting for him at the door, humbly implored the liberty of visiting so great a master of true wisdom. The lecturer hesitated a moment, when Rasselas put a purse of gold into his hand, which he received with a mixture of joy and wonder.

"I have found," said the prince at his return to Imlac, "a man who can teach all that is necessary to be known,

[1] **government of the passions** the sage's discourse and most of the other remarks in this chapter closely parallel statements in seventeenth- and eighteenth-century English versions of Stoic doctrines.

who, from the unshaken throne of rational fortitude, looks down on the scenes of life changing beneath him. He speaks, and attention watches his lips. He reasons, and conviction closes his periods.[2] This man shall be my future guide: I will learn his doctrines and imitate his life."

"Be not too hasty," said Imlac, "to trust, or to admire, the teachers of morality: they discourse like angels, but they live like men."

Rasselas, who could not conceive how any man could reason so forcibly without feeling the cogency of his own arguments, paid his visit in a few days, and was denied admission. He had now learned the power of money, and made his way by a piece of gold to the inner apartment, where he found the philosopher in a room half darkened, with his eyes misty and his face pale. "Sir," said he, "you are come at a time when all human friendship is useless; what I suffer cannot be remedied, what I have lost cannot be supplied. My daughter, my only daughter, from whose tenderness I expected all the comforts of my age, died last night of a fever. My views, my purposes, my hopes are at an end: I am now a lonely being disunited from society."

"Sir," said the prince, "mortality is an event by which a wise man can never be surprised: we know that death is always near, and it should therefore always be expected." "Young man," answered the philosopher, "you speak like one that has never felt the pangs of separation." "Have you then forgot the precepts," said Rasselas, "which you so powerfully enforced? Has wisdom no strength to arm the heart against calamity? Consider that external things are naturally variable, but truth and reason are always the same." "What comfort," said the mourner, "can truth and reason afford me? of what effect are they now but to tell me that my daughter will not be restored?" The prince, whose humanity would not suffer him to insult misery with reproof, went away convinced of the emptiness of rhetorical sound and the inefficacy of polished periods and studied sentences.[3]

[2] periods "a complete sentence from one full stop to another" (*Dictionary*)

[3] sentences "a maxim; an axiom, generally moral" (*Dictionary*)

CHAPTER XIX

A GLIMPSE OF PASTORAL LIFE

He was still eager upon the same enquiry; and, having heard of a hermit that lived near the lowest cataract of the Nile and filled the whole country with the fame of his sanctity, resolved to visit his retreat and enquire whether that felicity which public life could not afford was to be found in solitude; and whether a man whose age and virtue made him venerable could teach any peculiar art of shunning evils or enduring them.

Imlac and the princess agreed to accompany him, and, after the necessary preparations, they began their journey. Their way lay through fields where shepherds tended their flocks, and the lambs were playing upon the pasture. "This," said the poet, "is the life which has been often celebrated for its innocence and quiet: let us pass the heat of the day among the shepherds' tents, and know whether all our searches are not to terminate in pastoral simplicity."

The proposal pleased them, and they induced the shepherds, by small presents and familiar questions, to tell their opinion of their own state: they were so rude and ignorant, so little able to compare the good with the evil of the occupation, and so indistinct in their narratives and descriptions that very little could be learned from them. But it was evident that their hearts were cankered with discontent; that they considered themselves as condemned to labour for the luxury of the rich, and looked up with stupid malevolence toward those that were placed above them.

The princess pronounced with vehemence that she would never suffer these envious savages to be her companions, and that she should not soon be desirous of seeing any more specimens of rustic happiness; but could not believe that all the accounts of primeval pleasures were fabulous, and was yet in doubt whether life had anything that could be justly preferred to the placid gratifications of fields and woods. She hoped that the time would come when, with a few virtuous and elegant companions, she should gather flowers planted by her own hand, fondle the lambs of her own ewe, and listen, without care, among brooks and breezes, to one of her maidens reading in the shade.

CHAPTER XX

The Danger of Prosperity

On the next day they continued their journey till the heat compelled them to look round for shelter. At a small distance they saw a thick wood, which they no sooner entered than they perceived that they were approaching the habitations of men. The shrubs were diligently cut away to open walks where the shades were darkest; the boughs of opposite trees were artificially interwoven; seats of flowery turf were raised in vacant spaces, and a rivulet that wantoned [1] along the side of a winding path had its banks sometimes opened into small basins, and its stream sometimes obstructed by little mounds of stone heaped together to increase its murmurs.

They passed slowly through the wood, delighted with such unexpected accommodations, and entertained each other with conjecturing what, or who, he could be that, in those rude and unfrequented regions, had leisure and art for such harmless luxury.

As they advanced, they heard the sound of music and saw youths and virgins dancing in the grove; and, going still further, beheld a stately palace built upon a hill surrounded with woods. The laws of eastern hospitality allowed them to enter, and the master welcomed them like a man liberal and wealthy.

He was skilful enough in appearances soon to discern that they were no common guests, and spread his table with magnificence. The eloquence of Imlac caught his attention, and the lofty courtesy of the princess excited his respect. When they offered to depart he entreated

[1] **wantoned** "to revel; to play" (*Dictionary*)

their stay, and was the next day still more unwilling to dismiss them than before. They were easily persuaded to stop, and civility grew up in time to freedom and confidence.

The prince now saw all the domestics cheerful and all the face of nature smiling round the place, and could not forbear to hope that he should find here what he was seeking; but when he was congratulating the master upon his possessions, he answered with a sigh, "My condition has indeed the appearance of happiness, but appearances are delusive. My prosperity puts my life in danger; the Bassa[2] of Egypt is my enemy, incensed only by my wealth and popularity. I have been hitherto protected against him by the princess of the country; but, as the favour of the great is uncertain, I know not how soon my defenders may be persuaded to share the plunder with the Bassa. I have sent my treasures into a distant country, and, upon the first alarm, am prepared to follow them. Then will my enemies riot in my mansion and enjoy the gardens which I have planted."

They all joined in lamenting his danger and deprecating his exile; and the princess was so much disturbed with the tumult of grief and indignation that she retired to her apartment. They continued with their kind inviter a few days longer, and then went forward to find the hermit.

CHAPTER XXI

THE HAPPINESS OF SOLITUDE. THE HERMIT'S HISTORY

They came on the third day, by the direction of the peasants, to the hermit's cell: it was a cavern in the side of a mountain, over-shadowed with palm-trees; at such a distance from the cataract that nothing more was heard than a gentle uniform murmur,[1] such as composed the mind to pensive meditation, especially when it was assisted

[2] **Bassa** "a title of honour and command among the Turks; the viceroy of a province" (*Dictionary*)
[1] **murmur** several early discussions of the Nile refer to the rumor that its high cataracts fall with such a roar that they make the nearby inhabitants deaf

by the wind whistling among the branches. The first rude essay of nature had been so much improved by human labour that the cave contained several apartments, appropriated to different uses, and often afforded lodging to travellers whom darkness or tempests happened to overtake.

The hermit sat on a bench at the door, to enjoy the coolness of the evening. On one side lay a book with pens and papers, on the other mechanical instruments of various kinds. As they approached him unregarded, the princess observed that he had not the countenance of a man that had found, or could teach, the way to happiness.

They saluted him with great respect, which he repaid like a man not unaccustomed to the forms of courts. "My children," said he, "if you have lost your way, you shall be willingly supplied with such conveniences for the night as this cavern will afford. I have all that nature requires, and you will not expect delicacies in a hermit's cell."

They thanked him, and, entering, were pleased with the neatness and regularity of the place. The hermit set flesh and wine before them, though he fed only upon fruits and water. His discourse was cheerful without levity, and pious without enthusiasm.[2] He soon gained the esteem of his guests, and the princess repented of her hasty censure.

At last Imlac began thus: "I do not now wonder that your reputation is so far extended; we have heard at Cairo of your wisdom, and came hither to implore your direction for this young man and maiden in the *choice of life*."

"To him that lives well," answered the hermit, "every form of life is good; nor can I give any other rule for choice than to remove from all apparent evil."

"He will remove most certainly from evil," said the prince, "who shall devote himself to that solitude which you have recommended by your example."

"I have indeed lived fifteen years in solitude," said the hermit, "but have no desire that my example should gain any imitators. In my youth I professed arms, and was raised by degrees to the highest military rank. I have

---

[2] enthusiasm "a vain belief of private revelation; a vain confidence of divine favour or communication" (*Dictionary*)

traversed wide countries at the head of my troops, and seen many battles and sieges. At last, being disgusted by the preferments of a younger officer, and feeling that my vigour was beginning to decay, I resolved to close my life in peace, having found the world full of snares, discord, and misery. I had once escaped from the pursuit of the enemy by the shelter of this cavern and therefore chose it for my final residence. I employed artificers to form it into chambers, and stored it with all that I was likely to want.

"For some time after my retreat, I rejoiced like a tempest-beaten sailor at his entrance into the harbour, being delighted with the sudden change of the noise and hurry of war to stillness and repose. When the pleasure of novelty went away, I employed my hours in examining the plants which grow in the valley and the minerals which I collected from the rocks. But that enquiry is now grown tasteless and irksome. I have been for some time unsettled and distracted: my mind is disturbed with a thousand perplexities of doubt and vanities of imagination, which hourly prevail upon me because I have no opportunities of relaxation or diversion. I am sometimes ashamed to think that I could not secure myself from vice but by retiring from the exercise of virtue, and begin to suspect that I was rather impelled by resentment, than led by devotion, into solitude. My fancy riots in scenes of folly, and I lament that I have lost so much and have gained so little. In solitude, if I escape the example of bad men, I want likewise the counsel and conversation of the good. I have been long comparing the evils with the advantages of society, and resolve to return into the world tomorrow. The life of a solitary man will be certainly miserable, but not certainly devout."

They heard his resolution with surprise, but, after a short pause, offered to conduct him to Cairo. He dug up a considerable treasure which he had hid among the rocks, and accompanied them to the city, on which, as he approached it, he gazed with rapture.

CHAPTER XXII

The Happiness of a Life Led According to Nature [1]

Rasselas went often to an assembly of learned men who met at stated times to unbend their minds and compare their opinions. Their manners were somewhat coarse, but their conversation was instructive and their disputations acute, though sometimes too violent and often continued till neither controvertist remembered upon what question they began. Some faults were almost general among them: every one was desirous to dictate to the rest, and every one was pleased to hear the genius[2] or knowledge of another depreciated.

In this assembly Rasselas was relating his interview with the hermit, and the wonder with which he heard him censure a course of life which he had so deliberately chosen and so laudably followed. The sentiments of the hearers were various. Some were of opinion that the folly of his choice had been justly punished by condemnation to perpetual perseverance. One of the youngest among them, with great vehemence, pronounced him an hypocrite. Some talked of the right of society to the labour of individuals, and considered retirement as a desertion of duty. Others readily allowed that there was a time when the claims of the public were satisfied and when a man might properly sequester himself, to review his life and purify his heart.

One, who appeared more affected with the narrative

[1] **a life led according to nature** the ironical description of "a life led according to nature" closely resembles, in ideas and diction, portions of earlier discussions by English writers of the "law of nature," various conceptions of which constitute one of the persistent notions in the history of Western thought from classical to modern times. There appears to be no reason for supposing that, as is often suggested, Johnson had the particular doctrines of Rousseau in mind when he wrote this chapter.

[2] **genius** "mental power or faculties" (*Dictionary*)

than the rest, thought it likely that the hermit would, in a few years, go back to his retreat and, perhaps, if shame did not restrain, or death intercept him, return once more from his retreat into the world: "For the hope of happiness," said he, "is so strongly impressed that the longest experience is not able to efface it. Of the present state, whatever it be, we feel, and are forced to confess, the misery, yet, when the same state is again at a distance, imagination paints it as desirable. But the time will surely come when desire will be no longer our torment, and no man shall be wretched but by his own fault."

"This," said a philosopher who had heard him with tokens of great impatience, "is the present condition of a wise man. The time is already come when none are wretched but by their own fault. Nothing is more idle than to enquire after happiness, which nature has kindly placed within our reach. The way to be happy is to live according to nature, in obedience to that universal and unalterable law with which every heart is originally impressed; which is not written on it by precept but engraven by destiny, not instilled by education but infused at our nativity. He that lives according to nature will suffer nothing from the delusions of hope or importunities of desire: he will receive and reject with equability of temper; and act or suffer as the reason of things shall alternately prescribe. Other men may amuse themselves with subtle definitions or intricate ratiocination. Let them learn to be wise by easier means: let them observe the hind of the forest and the linnet of the grove: let them consider the life of animals, whose motions are regulated by instinct; they obey their guide and are happy. Let us therefore, at length, cease to dispute and learn to live; throw away the incumbrance of precepts, which they who utter them with so much pride and pomp do not understand, and carry with us this simple and intelligible maxim, That deviation from nature is deviation from happiness."

When he had spoken, he looked round him with a placid air, and enjoyed the consciousness of his own beneficence. "Sir," said the prince with great modesty, "as I, like all the rest of mankind, am desirous of felicity, my closest attention has been fixed upon your discourse: I doubt not the truth of a position which a man so learned has so confidently advanced. Let me only know what it is to live according to nature."

"When I find young men so humble and so docile," said the philosopher, "I can deny them no information which my studies have enabled me to afford. To live according to nature is to act always with due regard to the fitness arising from the relations and qualities of causes and effects; to concur with the great and unchangeable scheme of universal felicity; to co-operate with the general disposition and tendency of the present system of things."

The prince soon found that this was one of the sages whom he should understand less as he heard him longer. He therefore bowed and was silent, and the philosopher, supposing him satisfied and the rest vanquished, rose up and departed with the air of a man that had co-operated with the present system.

CHAPTER XXIII

The Prince and His Sister Divide Between Them the Work of Observation

Rasselas returned home full of reflexions, doubtful how to direct his future steps. Of the way to happiness he found the learned and simple equally ignorant; but, as he was yet young, he flattered himself that he had time remaining for more experiments and further enquiries. He communicated to Imlac his observations and his doubts, but was answered by him with new doubts and remarks that gave him no comfort. He therefore discoursed more frequently and freely with his sister, who had yet the same hope with himself, and always assisted him to give some reason why, though he had been hitherto frustrated, he might succeed at last.

"We have hitherto," said she, "known but little of the world: we have never yet been either great or mean. In our own country, though we had royalty, we had no power, and in this we have not yet seen the private recesses of domestic peace. Imlac favours not our search lest

we should in time find him mistaken. We will divide the
task between us: you shall try what is to be found in the
splendour of courts, and I will range the shades of humbler
life. Perhaps command and authority may be the supreme
blessings, as they afford most opportunities of doing good:
or, perhaps, what this world can give may be found in the
modest habitations of middle fortune; too low for great
designs and too high for penury and distress."

CHAPTER XXIV

THE PRINCE EXAMINES THE HAPPINESS OF HIGH STATIONS

Rasselas applauded the design, and appeared next day
with a splendid retinue at the court of the Bassa. He was
soon distinguished for his magnificence, and admitted,
as a prince whose curiosity had brought him from distant
countries, to an intimacy with the great officers, and frequent conversation with the Bassa himself.

He was at first inclined to believe that the man must
be pleased with his own condition whom all approached
with reverence and heard with obedience, and who had
the power to extend his edicts to a whole kingdom. "There
can be no pleasure," said he, "equal to that of feeling at
once the joy of thousands all made happy by wise administration. Yet, since, by the law of subordination, this
sublime delight can be in one nation but the lot of one,
it is surely reasonable to think that there is some satisfaction more popular and accessible, and that millions can
hardly be subjected to the will of a single man only to
fill his particular breast with incommunicable content."

These thoughts were often in his mind, and he found
no solution of the difficulty. But as presents and civilities
gained him more familiarity, he found that almost every
man who stood high in employment hated all the rest,
and was hated by them, and that their lives were a continual succession of plots and detections, stratagems and
escapes, faction and treachery. Many of those who surrounded the Bassa were sent only to watch and report his

conduct; every tongue was muttering censure, and every
eye was searching for a fault.

At last the letters of revocation arrived, the Bassa was
carried in chains to Constantinople, and his name was
mentioned no more.

"What are we now to think of the prerogatives of
power," said Rasselas to his sister; "is it without any ef-
ficacy to good? or is the subordinate degree only dangerous and the supreme safe and glorious? Is the Sultan the
only happy man in his dominions? or is the Sultan himself
subject to the torments of suspicion and the dread of
enemies?"

In a short time the second Bassa was deposed. The
Sultan that had advanced him was murdered by the Janisaries,[1] and his successor had other views and different
favourites.

CHAPTER XXV

THE PRINCESS PURSUES HER ENQUIRY
WITH MORE DILIGENCE THAN SUCCESS

The princess, in the meantime, insinuated [1] herself into
many families; for there are few doors through which
liberality, joined with good humour, cannot find its way.
The daughters of many houses were airy[2] and cheerful,
but Nekayah had been too long accustomed to the conversation of Imlac and her brother to be much pleased
with childish levity and prattle which had no meaning.
She found their thoughts narrow, their wishes low, and
their merriment often artificial. Their pleasures, poor as
they were, could not be preserved pure, but were embittered by petty competitions and worthless emulation.

---

[1] Janisaries "one of the guards of the Turkish king" (*Dictionary*)

[1] insinuated "to push gently into favour or regard: commonly
with the reciprocal pronoun" (*Dictionary*)

[2] airy "gay; sprightly; full of mirth; . . . light of heart" (*Dictionary*)

They were always jealous of the beauty of each other; of a quality to which solicitude can add nothing, and from which detraction can take nothing away. Many were in love with triflers like themselves, and many fancied that they were in love when in truth they were only idle. Their affection was seldom fixed on sense or virtue, and therefore seldom ended but in vexation. Their grief, however, like their joy, was transient; everything floated in their mind unconnected with the past or future, so that one desire easily gave way to another, as a second stone cast into the water effaces and confounds[3] the circles of the first.

With these girls she played as with inoffensive animals, and found them proud of her countenance[4] and weary of her company.

But her purpose was to examine more deeply, and her affability easily persuaded the hearts that were swelling with sorrow to discharge their secrets in her ear: and those whom hope flattered, or prosperity delighted, often courted her to partake their pleasures.

The princess and her brother commonly met in the evening in a private summerhouse on the bank of the Nile, and related to each other the occurrences of the day. As they were sitting together, the princess cast her eyes upon the river that flowed before her. "Answer," said she, "great father of waters, thou that rollest thy floods through eighty nations, to the invocations of the daughter of thy native king. Tell me if thou waterest, through all thy course, a single habitation from which thou dost not hear the murmurs of complaint?"

"You are then," said Rasselas, "not more successful in private houses than I have been in courts." "I have, since the last partition of our provinces,"[5] said the princess, "enabled myself to enter familiarly into many families where there was the fairest show of prosperity and peace, and know not one house that is not haunted by some fury that destroys its quiet.

[3] **confounds** "to mingle things so that their several forms or natures cannot be discerned" (*Dictionary*)

[4] **countenance** "patronage; appearance of favour; . . . support" (*Dictionary*)

[5] **provinces** "the proper office or business of any one" (*Dictionary*)

"I did not seek ease among the poor, because I concluded that there it could not be found. But I saw many poor whom I had supposed to live in affluence. Poverty has, in large cities, very different appearances: it is often concealed in splendour and often in extravagance. It is the care of a very great part of mankind to conceal their indigence from the rest: they support themselves by temporary expedients, and every day is lost in contriving for the morrow.

"This, however, was an evil which, though frequent, I saw with less pain because I could relieve it. Yet some have refused my bounties; more offended with my quickness to detect their wants than pleased with my readiness to succour them: and others, whose exigencies compelled them to admit my kindness, have never been able to forgive their benefactress. Many, however, have been sincerely grateful without the ostentation of gratitude or the hope of other favours."

CHAPTER XXVI

THE PRINCESS CONTINUES HER REMARKS UPON PRIVATE LIFE

Nekayah perceiving her brother's attention fixed, proceeded in her narrative.

"In families, where there is or is not poverty, there is commonly discord: if a kingdom be, as Imlac tells us, a great family, a family likewise is a little kingdom, torn with factions and exposed to revolutions. An unpracticed observer expects the love of parents and children to be constant and equal; but this kindness seldom continues beyond the years of infancy: in a short time the children become rivals to their parents. Benefits are allayed [1] by reproaches, and gratitude debased by envy.

"Parents and children seldom act in concert: each child endeavours to appropriate the esteem or fondness of the parents, and the parents, with yet less temptation,

---

[1] allayed "to join any thing to another, so as to abate its predominant qualities" (*Dictionary*)

betray each other to their children; thus some place their confidence in the father and some in the mother, and, by degrees, the house is filled with artifices and feuds.

"The opinions of children and parents, of the young and the old, are naturally opposite, by the contrary effects of hope and despondence, of expectation and experience, without crime or folly on either side. The colours of life in youth and age appear different, as the face of nature in spring and winter. And how can children credit the assertions of parents which their own eyes show them to be false?

"Few parents act in such a manner as much to enforce their maxims by the credit of their lives. The old man trusts wholly to slow contrivance and gradual progression: the youth expects to force his way by genius, vigour, and precipitance. The old man pays regard to riches, and the youth reverences virtue. The old man deifies prudence: the youth commits himself to magnanimity and chance. The young man, who intends no ill, believes that none is intended, and therefore acts with openness and candour:[2] but his father, having suffered the injuries of fraud, is impelled to suspect, and too often allured to practice it. Age looks with anger on the temerity of youth, and youth with contempt on the scrupulosity of age. Thus parents and children, for the greatest part, live on to love less and less: and if those whom nature has thus closely united are the torments of each other, where shall we look for tenderness and consolation?"

"Surely," said the prince, "you must have been unfortunate in your choice of acquaintance: I am unwilling to believe that the most tender of all relations is thus impeded in its effects by natural necessity."

"Domestic discord," answered she, "is not inevitably and fatally[3] necessary; but yet is not easily avoided. We seldom see that a whole family is virtuous: the good and evil cannot well agree; and the evil can yet less agree with one another: even the virtuous fall sometimes to variance

[2] **candour** "sweetness of temper; purity of mind; . . . kindness" (*Dictionary*)

[3] **fatally** "by the decree of fate; by inevitable and invincible determination" (*Dictionary*)

when their virtues are of different kinds and tending to extremes. In general, those parents have most reverence who most deserve it: for he that lives well cannot be despised.

"Many other evils infest private life. Some are the slaves of servants whom they have trusted with their affairs. Some are kept in continual anxiety to the caprice of rich relations, whom they cannot please and dare not offend. Some husbands are imperious and some wives perverse: and, as it is always more easy to do evil than good, though the wisdom or virtue of one can very rarely make many happy, the folly or vice of one may often make many miserable."

"If such be the general effect of marriage," said the prince, "I shall, for the future, think it dangerous to connect my interest with that of another, lest I should be unhappy by my partner's fault."

"I have met," said the princess, "with many who live single for that reason; but I never found that their prudence ought to raise envy. They dream away their time without friendship, without fondness, and are driven to rid themselves of the day for which they have no use, by childish amusements or vicious delights. They act as beings under the constant sense of some known inferiority that fills their minds with rancour and their tongues with censure. They are peevish at home and malevolent abroad; and, as the outlaws of human nature, make it their business and their pleasure to disturb that society which debars them from its privileges. To live without feeling or exciting sympathy, to be fortunate without adding to the felicity of others, or afflicted without tasting the balm of pity, is a state more gloomy than solitude: it is not retreat but exclusion from mankind. Marriage has many pains, but celibacy has no pleasures."

"What then is to be done?" said Rasselas; "the more we enquire, the less we can resolve. Surely he is most likely to please himself that has no other inclination to regard."

CHAPTER XXVII

DISQUISITION UPON GREATNESS

The conversation had a short pause. The prince, having considered his sister's observations, told her that she had surveyed life with prejudice and supposed misery where she did not find it. "Your narrative," says he, "throws yet a darker gloom upon the prospects of futurity: the predictions of Imlac were but faint sketches of the evils painted by Nekayah. I have been lately convinced that quiet is not the daughter of grandeur or of power: that her presence is not to be bought by wealth nor enforced by conquest. It is evident that as any man acts in a wider compass he must be more exposed to opposition from enmity or miscarriage from chance; whoever has many to please or to govern must use the ministry of many agents, some of whom will be wicked, and some ignorant; by some he will be misled and by others betrayed. If he gratifies one he will offend another: those that are not favoured will think themselves injured; and, since favours can be conferred but upon few, the greater number will be always discontented."

"The discontent," said the princess, "which is thus unreasonable I hope that I shall always have spirit to despise, and you power to repress."

"Discontent," answered Rasselas, "will not always be without reason under the most just or vigilant administration of public affairs. None, however attentive, can always discover that merit which indigence or faction may happen to obscure; and none, however powerful, can always reward it. Yet he that sees inferior desert advanced above him will naturally impute that preference to partiality or caprice; and, indeed, it can scarcely be hoped that any man, however magnanimous by nature or exalted by condition, will be able to persist forever in fixed and inexorable justice of distribution: he will sometimes indulge his own affections and sometimes those of his favourites; he will permit some to please him who can never serve him; he will discover in those whom he loves qualities which in reality they do not possess; and to those from whom he receives pleasure he will in his turn endeavour to give it. Thus will recommendations sometimes prevail which were purchased by money, or by the more destructive bribery of flattery and servility."

"He that has much to do will do something wrong, and of that wrong must suffer the consequences; and, if it were possible that he should always act rightly, yet when such numbers are to judge of his conduct, the bad will censure and obstruct him by malevolence, and the good sometimes by mistake.

"The highest stations cannot therefore hope to be the abodes of happiness, which I would willingly believe to have fled from thrones and palaces to seats of humble privacy and placid obscurity. For what can hinder the satisfaction, or intercept the expectations, of him whose abilities are adequate to his employments, who sees with his own eyes the whole circuit of his influence, who chooses by his own knowledge all whom he trusts, and whom none are tempted to deceive by hope or fear? Surely he has nothing to do but to love and to be loved, to be virtuous and to be happy."

"Whether perfect happiness would be procured by perfect goodness," said Nekayah, "this world will never afford an opportunity of deciding. But this, at least, may be maintained, that we do not always find visible happiness in proportion to visible virtue. All natural and almost all political evils are incident alike to the bad and good: they are confounded in the misery of a famine, and not much distinguished in the fury of a faction; they sink together in a tempest, and are driven together from their country by invaders. All that virtue can afford is quietness of conscience, a steady prospect of a happier state; this may enable us to endure calamity with patience; but remember that patience must suppose pain."

CHAPTER XXVIII

Rasselas and Nekayah Continue Their Conversation

"Dear princess," said Rasselas, "you fall into the common errors of exaggeratory declamation[1] by producing, in a familiar disquisition, examples of national calamities and scenes of extensive misery which are found in books rather than in the world and which, as they are horrid,[2] are ordained to be rare. Let us not imagine evils which we do not feel, nor injure life by misrepresentations. I cannot bear that querulous eloquence which threatens every city with a siege like that of Jerusalem,[3] that makes famine attend on every flight of locusts, and suspends pestilence on the wing of every blast that issues from the south.

"On necessary and inevitable evils, which overwhelm kingdoms at once, all disputation is vain: when they happen they must be endured. But it is evident that these bursts of universal distress are more dreaded than felt: thousands and ten thousands flourish in youth and wither in age, without the knowledge of any other than domestic evils, and share the same pleasures and vexations whether their kings are mild or cruel, whether the armies of their country pursue their enemies, or retreat before them. While courts are disturbed with intestine competitions, and ambassadors are negotiating in foreign countries, the smith still plies his anvil and the husbandman drives his plow forward; the necessaries of life are required and obtained, and the successive business of the seasons continues to make its wonted revolutions.

"Let us cease to consider what, perhaps, may never happen, and what, when it shall happen, will laugh at

[1] declamation "a discourse addressed to the passions; an harangue" (*Dictionary*)
[2] horrid "hideous; dreadful; shocking" (*Dictionary*)
[3] Jerusalem in 70 A.D. Emperor Titus beseiged, captured, and destroyed Jerusalem

human speculation. We will not endeavour to modify the motions of the elements or to fix the destiny of kingdoms. It is our business to consider what beings like us may perform; each labouring for his own happiness by promoting within his circle, however narrow, the happiness of others.

"Marriage is evidently the dictate of nature; men and women were made to be companions of each other, and therefore I cannot be persuaded but that marriage is one of the means of happiness."

"I know not," said the princess, "whether marriage be more than one of the innumerable modes of human misery. When I see and reckon the various forms of connubial infelicity, the unexpected causes of lasting discord, the diversities of temper, the oppositions of opinion, the rude collisions of contrary desire where both are urged by violent impulses, the obstinate contests of disagreeing virtues where both are supported by consciousness of good intention, I am sometimes disposed to think with the severer casuists of most nations that marriage is rather permitted than approved, and that none, but by the instigation of a passion too much indulged, entangle themselves with indissoluble compacts."

"You seem to forget," replied Rasselas, "that you have, even now, represented celibacy as less happy than marriage. Both conditions may be bad, but they cannot both be worst. Thus it happens when wrong opinions are entertained, that they mutually destroy each other and leave the mind open to truth."

"I did not expect," answered the princess, "to hear that imputed to falsehood which is the consequence only of frailty. To the mind, as to the eye, it is difficult to compare with exactness objects vast in their extent and various in their parts. Where we see or conceive the whole at once we readily note the discriminations and decide the preference: but of two systems, of which neither can be surveyed by any human being in its full compass of magnitude and multiplicity of complication, where is the wonder that judging of the whole by parts I am alternately affected by one and the other as either presses on my memory or fancy? We differ from ourselves just as we differ from each other when we see only part of the question, as in the multifarious relations of politics and morality: but when we perceive the whole at once, as in numerical computations, all agree in one judgment, and none ever varies his opinion."

"Let us not add," said the prince, "to the other evils of life the bitterness of controversy, nor endeavour to vie with each other in subtilties of argument. We are employed in a search of which both are equally to enjoy the success or suffer by the miscarriage. It is therefore fit that we assist each other. You surely conclude too hastily from the infelicity of marriage against its institution; will not the misery of life prove equally that life cannot be the gift of heaven? The world must be peopled by marriage or peopled without it."

"How the world is to be peopled," returned Nekayah, "is not my care and needs not be yours. I see no danger that the present generation should omit to leave successors behind them: we are not now enquiring for the world, but for ourselves."

CHAPTER XXIX

THE DEBATE ON MARRIAGE CONTINUED

"The good of the whole," says Rasselas, "is the same with the good of all its parts. If marriage be best for mankind it must be evidently best for individuals, or a permanent and necessary duty must be the cause of evil, and some must be inevitably sacrificed to the convenience of others. In the estimate which you have made of the two states, it appears that the incommodities of a single life are, in a great measure, necessary and certain, but those of the conjugal state accidental and avoidable.

"I cannot forbear to flatter myself that prudence and benevolence will make marriage happy. The general folly of mankind is the cause of general complaint. What can be expected but disappointment and repentance from a choice made in the immaturity of youth, in the ardour of desire, without judgment, without foresight, without enquiry after conformity of opinions, similarity of manners, rectitude of judgment, or purity of sentiment.

"Such is the common process of marriage. A youth and maiden meeting by chance, or brought together by artifice, exchange glances, reciprocate civilities, go home, and dream of one another. Having little to divert attention or diversify thought, they find themselves uneasy when they are apart, and therefore conclude that they shall be happy together. They marry, and discover what nothing but voluntary blindness had before concealed; they wear out life in altercations and charge nature with cruelty.

"From those early marriages proceeds likewise the rivalry of parents and children: the son is eager to enjoy the world before the father is willing to forsake it, and there is hardly room at once for two generations. The daughter begins to bloom before the mother can be content to fade, and neither can forbear to wish for the absence of the other.

"Surely all these evils may be avoided by that deliberation and delay which prudence prescribes to irrevocable choice. In the variety and jollity of youthful pleasures life may be well enough supported without the help of a partner. Longer time will increase experience, and wider views will allow better opportunities of enquiry and selection: one advantage, at least, will be certain; the parents will be visibly older than their children."

"What reason cannot collect," said Nekayah, "and what experiment has not yet taught, can be known only from the report of others. I have been told that late marriages are not eminently happy. This is a question too important to be neglected, and I have often proposed it to those whose accuracy of remark and comprehensiveness of knowledge made their suffrages[1] worthy of regard. They have generally determined that it is dangerous for a man and woman to suspend[2] their fate upon each other at a time when opinions are fixed and habits are established; when friendships have been contracted on both sides, when life has been planned into method, and the mind has long enjoyed the contemplation of its own prospects.

"It is scarcely possible that two travelling through the world under the conduct of chance should have been both

[1] suffrages "voice given in a controverted point" (*Dictionary*)
[2] suspend "to make to depend upon" (*Dictionary*)

directed to the same path, and it will not often happen that either will quit the track which custom has made pleasing. When the desultory levity of youth has settled into regularity, it is soon succeeded by pride ashamed to yield or obstinacy delighting to contend. And even though mutual esteem produces mutual desire to please, time itself, as it modifies unchangeably the external mien, determines likewise the direction of the passions and gives an inflexible rigidity to the manners. Long customs are not easily broken: he that attempts to change the course of his own life very often labours in vain; and how shall we do that for others which we are seldom able to do for ourselves?"

"But surely," interposed the prince, "you suppose the chief motive of choice forgotten or neglected. Whenever I shall seek a wife, it shall be my first question whether she be willing to be led by reason?"

"Thus it is," said Nekayah, "that philosophers are deceived. There are a thousand familiar disputes which reason never can decide; questions that elude investigation and make logic ridiculous; cases where something must be done, and where little can be said. Consider the state of mankind, and enquire how few can be supposed to act upon any occasions, whether small or great, with all the reasons of action present to their minds. Wretched would be the pair above all names of wretchedness who should be doomed to adjust by reason every morning all the minute detail of a domestic day.

"Those who marry at an advanced age will probably escape the encroachments of their children; but, in diminution of this advantage, they will be likely to leave them, ignorant and helpless, to a guardian's mercy: or, if that should not happen, they must at least go out of the world before they see those whom they love best either wise or great.

"From their children, if they have less to fear, they have less also to hope, and they lose, without equivalent, the joys of early love and the convenience of uniting with manners pliant and minds susceptible of new impressions, which might wear away their dissimilitudes by long cohabitation, as soft bodies, by continual attrition, conform their surfaces to each other.

"I believe it will be found that those who marry late are best pleased with their children, and those who marry early with their partners."

"The union of these two affections," said Rasselas, "would produce all that could be wished. Perhaps there is a time when marriage might unite them, a time neither too early for the father nor too late for the husband."

"Every hour," answered the princess, "confirms my prejudice in favour of the position so often uttered by the mouth of Imlac, 'That nature sets her gifts on the right hand and on the left.' Those conditions which flatter hope and attract desire are so constituted that, as we approach one, we recede from another. There are goods so opposed that we cannot seize both, but, by too much prudence, may pass between them at too great a distance to reach either. This is often the fate of long consideration; he does nothing who endeavours to do more than is allowed to humanity. Flatter not yourself with contrarieties of pleasure. Of the blessings set before you make your choice, and be content. No man can taste the fruits of autumn while he is delighting his scent with the flowers of the spring: no man can, at the same time, fill his cup from the source and from the mouth of the Nile."

CHAPTER XXX

Imlac Enters and Changes the Conversation

Here Imlac entered and interrupted them. "Imlac," said Rasselas, "I have been taking from the princess the dismal history of private life, and am almost discouraged from further search."

"It seems to me," said Imlac, "that while you are making the choice of life, you neglect to live. You wander about a single city, which, however large and diversified, can now afford few novelties, and forget that you are in a country famous among the earliest monarchies for the power and wisdom of its inhabitants; a country where the sciences first dawned that illuminate the world, and beyond which the arts cannot be traced of civil society or domestic life.

"The old Egyptians have left behind them monuments of industry and power before which all European magnificence is confessed to fade away. The ruins of their architecture are the schools of modern builders, and from the wonders which time has spared we may conjecture, though uncertainly, what it has destroyed."

"My curiosity," said Rasselas, "does not very strongly lead me to survey piles of stone or mounds of earth; my business is with man. I came hither not to measure fragments of temples or trace choked aqueducts, but to look upon the various scenes of the present world."

"The things that are now before us," said the princess, "require attention and deserve it. What have I to do with the heroes or the monuments of ancient times? with times which never can return, and heroes whose form of life was different from all that the present condition of mankind requires or allows."

"To know any thing," returned the poet, "we must know its effects; to see men we must see their works, that we may learn what reason has dictated or passion has incited, and find what are the most powerful motives of action. To judge rightly of the present we must oppose it to the past; for all judgment is comparative, and of the future nothing can be known. The truth is that no mind is much employed upon the present: recollection and anticipation fill up almost all our moments. Our passions are joy and grief, love and hatred, hope and fear. Of joy and grief the past is the object, and the future of hope and fear; even love and hatred respect the past, for the cause must have been before the effect.

"The present state of things is the consequence of the former, and it is natural to inquire what were the sources of the good that we enjoy, or of the evil that we suffer. If we act only for ourselves, to neglect the study of history is not prudent: if we are entrusted with the care of others, it is not just. Ignorance, when it is voluntary, is criminal; and he may properly be charged with evil who refused to learn how he might prevent it.

"There is no part of history so generally useful as that

which relates the progress of the human mind, the gradual improvement of reason, the successive advances of science, the vicissitudes of learning and ignorance, which are the light and darkness of thinking beings, the extinction and resuscitation of arts, and the revolutions of the intellectual world. If accounts of battles and invasions are peculiarly the business of princes, the useful or elegant arts are not to be neglected; those who have kingdoms to govern have understandings to cultivate.

"Example is always more efficacious than precept. A soldier is formed in war, and a painter must copy pictures. In this, contemplative life has the advantage: great actions are seldom seen, but the labours of art are always at hand for those who desire to know what art has been able to perform.

"When the eye or the imagination is struck with any uncommon work the next transition of an active mind is to the means by which it was performed. Here begins the true use of such contemplation; we enlarge our comprehension by new ideas, and perhaps recover some art lost to mankind, or learn what is less perfectly known in our own country. At least we compare our own with former times and either rejoice at our improvements, or, what is the first motion towards good, discover our defects."

"I am willing," said the prince, "to see all that can deserve my search." "And I," said the princess, "shall rejoice to learn something of the manners of antiquity."

"The most pompous[1] monument of Egyptian greatness, and one of the most bulky works of manual industry," said Imlac, "are the pyramids; fabrics raised before the time of history, and of which the earliest narratives afford us only uncertain traditions. Of these the greatest is still standing, very little injured by time."

"Let us visit them tomorrow," said Nekayah. "I have often heard of the Pyramids, and shall not rest till I have seen them within and without with my own eyes."

---

[1] **pompous** "splendid; magnificent; grand" (*Dictionary*)

CHAPTER XXXI

They Visit the Pyramids

The resolution being thus taken, they set out the next day. They laid tents upon their camels, being resolved to stay among the pyramids till their curiosity was fully satisfied. They travelled gently, turned aside to every thing remarkable, stopped from time to time and conversed with the inhabitants, and observed the various appearances of towns ruined and inhabited, of wild and cultivated nature.

When they came to the great pyramid they were astonished at the extent of the base and the height of the top. Imlac explained to them the principles upon which the pyramidal form was chosen for a fabric intended to co-extend its duration with that of the world: he showed that its gradual diminution gave it such stability as defeated all the common attacks of the elements and could scarcely be overthrown by earthquakes themselves, the least resistible of natural violence. A concussion that should shatter the pyramid would threaten the dissolution of the continent.

They measured all its dimensions, and pitched their tents at its foot. Next day they prepared to enter its interior apartments, and having hired the common guides climbed up to the first passage, when the favourite of the princess, looking into the cavity, stepped back and trembled. "Pekuah," said the princess, "of what art thou afraid?" "Of the narrow entrance," answered the lady, "and of the dreadful gloom. I dare not enter a place which must surely be inhabited by unquiet souls. The original possessors of these dreadful vaults will start up before us and, perhaps, shut us in forever." She spoke, and threw her arms round the neck of her mistress.

"If all your fear be of apparitions," said the prince, "I will promise you safety: there is no danger from the dead; he that is once buried will be seen no more."

"That the dead are seen no more," said Imlac, "I will not undertake to maintain against the concurrent and unvaried testimony of all ages and of all nations. There is no people, rude or learned, among whom apparitions of the dead are not related and believed. This opinion, which, perhaps, prevails as far as human nature is diffused, could become universal only by its truth: those that never heard of one another would not have agreed in a tale which nothing but experience can make credible. That it is doubted by single cavillers can very little weaken the general evidence, and some who deny it with their tongues confess it by their fears.

"Yet I do not mean to add new terrors to those which have already seized upon Pekuah. There can be no reason why spectres should haunt the pyramid more than other places, or why they should have power or will to hurt innocence and purity. Our entrance is no violation of their privileges; we can take nothing from them, how then can we offend them?"

"My dear Pekuah," said the princess, "I will always go before you, and Imlac shall follow you. Remember that you are the companion of the princess of Abyssinia."

"If the princess is pleased that her servant should die," returned the lady, "let her command some death less dreadful than enclosure in this horrid cavern. You know I dare not disobey you: I must go if you command me; but, if I once enter, I never shall come back."

The princess saw that her fear was too strong for expostulation or reproof, and embracing her, told her that she should stay in the tent till their return. Pekuah was yet not satisfied, but entreated the princess not to pursue so dreadful a purpose as that of entering the recesses of the pyramid. "Though I cannot teach courage," said Nekayah, "I must not learn cowardice; nor leave at last undone what I came hither only to do."

CHAPTER XXXII

They Enter the Pyramid

Pekuah descended to the tents, and the rest entered the pyramid: they passed through the galleries, surveyed the vaults of marble, and examined the chest in which the body of the founder[1] is supposed to have been reposited. They then sat down in one of the most spacious chambers to rest a while before they attempted to return.

"We have now," said Imlac, "gratified our minds with an exact view of the greatest work of man, except the wall of China.

"Of the wall it is very easy to assign the motives. It secured a wealthy and timorous nation from the incursions of Barbarians, whose unskilfulness in arts made it easier for them to supply their wants by rapine than by industry, and who from time to time poured in upon the habitations of peaceful commerce, as vultures descend upon domestic fowl. Their celerity and fierceness made the wall necessary, and their ignorance made it efficacious.

"But for the pyramids no reason has ever been given adequate to the cost and labour of the work. The narrowness of the chambers proves that it could afford no retreat from enemies, and treasures might have been reposited at far less expence with equal security. It seems to have been erected only in compliance with that hunger of imagination which preys incessantly upon life and must be always appeased by some employment. Those who have already all that they can enjoy, must enlarge their desires. He that has built for use, till use is supplied, must begin to build for vanity, and extend his plan to the utmost power of human performance, that he may not be soon reduced to form another wish.

"I consider this mighty structure as a monument of the insufficiency of human enjoyments. A king whose power is unlimited, and whose treasures surmount all real and imaginary wants, is compelled to solace, by the erection of a pyramid, the satiety of dominion and tastelessness of pleasures, and to amuse the tediousness of declining life, by seeing thousands labouring without end, and one stone, for no purpose, laid upon another. Whoever thou art that, not content with a moderate condition, imaginest happiness in royal magnificence and dreamest that command or riches can feed the appetite of novelty with perpetual gratifications, survey the pyramids and confess thy folly!"

[1] **founder** "a builder; one who raises an edifice" (*Dictionary*); specifically Cheops (*c.* 2900-2877 B.C.)

CHAPTER XXXIII

THE PRINCESS MEETS WITH AN UNEXPECTED MISFORTUNE

They rose up, and returned through the cavity at which they had entered, and the princess prepared for her favourite a long narrative of dark labyrinths and costly rooms, and of the different impressions which the varieties of the way had made upon her. But when they came to their train, they found everyone silent and dejected: the men discovered shame and fear in their countenances, and the women were weeping in the tents.

What had happened they did not try to conjecture but immediately enquired. "You had scarcely entered into the pyramid," said one of the attendants, "when a troop of Arabs rushed upon us: we were too few to resist them and too slow to escape. They were about to search the tents, set us on our camels, and drive us along before them, when the approach of some Turkish horsemen put them to flight; but they seized the lady Pekuah with her two maids and carried them away: the Turks are now pursuing them by our instigation, but I fear they will not be able to overtake them."

The princess was overpowered with surprise and grief. Rasselas, in the first heat of his resentment, ordered his servants to follow him, and prepared to pursue the robbers with his sabre in his hand. "Sir," said Imlac, "what can you hope from violence or valour? the Arabs are mounted on horses trained to battle and retreat; we have only beasts of burden. By leaving our present station we may lose the princess, but cannot hope to regain Pekuah."

In a short time the Turks returned, having not been able to reach the enemy. The princess burst out into new lamentations, and Rasselas could scarcely forbear to reproach them with cowardice; but Imlac was of opinion that the escape of the Arabs was no addition to their misfortune, for, perhaps, they would have killed their captives rather than have resigned them.

CHAPTER XXXIV

They Return to Cairo without Pekuah

There was nothing to be hoped from longer stay. They returned to Cairo repenting of their curiosity, censuring the negligence of the government, lamenting their own rashness which had neglected to procure a guard, imagining many expedients by which the loss of Pekuah might have been prevented, and resolving to do something for her recovery, though none could find anything proper to be done.

Nekayah retired to her chamber, where her women attempted to comfort her by telling her that all had their troubles, and that lady Pekuah had enjoyed much happiness in the world for a long time and might reasonably expect a change of fortune. They hoped that some good would befall her wheresoever she was, and that their mistress would find another friend who might supply her place.

The princess made them no answer, and they continued the form of condolence, not much grieved in their hearts that the favourite was lost.

Next day the prince presented to the Bassa a memorial of the wrong which he had suffered, and a petition for redress. The Bassa threatened to punish the robbers, but did not attempt to catch them, nor, indeed, could any account or description be given by which he might direct the pursuit.

It soon appeared that nothing would be done by authority. Governors, being accustomed to hear of more crimes than they can punish and more wrongs than they can redress, set themselves at ease by indiscriminate negligence, and presently forget the request when they lose sight of the petitioner.

Imlac then endeavoured to gain some intelligence by private agents. He found many who pretended to an exact knowledge of all the haunts of the Arabs, and to regular correspondence with their chiefs, and who readily undertook the recovery of Pekuah. Of these, some were furnished with money for their journey, and came back no more; some were liberally paid for accounts which a few days discovered to be false. But the princess would not suffer any means, however improbable, to be left untried. While she was doing something she kept her hope alive. As one expedient failed, another was suggested; when one messenger returned unsuccessful, another was despatched to a different quarter.

Two months had now passed, and of Pekuah nothing had been heard; the hopes which they had endeavoured to raise in each other grew more languid, and the princess, when she saw nothing more to be tried, sunk[1] down inconsolable in hopeless dejection. A thousand times she reproached herself with the easy compliance by which she permitted her favourite to stay behind her. "Had not my fondness," said she, "lessened my authority, Pekuah had not dared to talk of her terrors. She ought to have feared me more than spectres. A severe look would have overpowered her; a peremptory command would have compelled obedience. Why did foolish indulgence prevail upon me? Why did I not speak and refuse to hear?"

"Great princess," said Imlac, "do not reproach yourself for your virtue, or consider that as blameable by which evil has accidentally been caused. Your tenderness for the timidity of Pekuah was generous and kind. When we act according to our duty, we commit the event to him by whose laws our actions are governed, and who will suffer none to be finally punished for obedience. When, in prospect of some good, whether natural or moral, we break the rules prescribed us, we withdraw from the direction of superior wisdom and take all consequences upon ourselves. Man cannot so far know the connection of causes and events as that he may venture to do wrong in order to do right. When we pursue our end by lawful means, we may always console our miscarriage by the hope of future recompense. When we consult only our own policy and attempt to find a nearer way to good by overleaping the settled boundaries of right and wrong, we cannot be happy even by success, because we cannot

[1] sunk "the preterite and participle passive of *sink*" (*Dictionary*)

escape the consciousness of our fault; but, if we miscarry, the disappointment is irremediably embittered. How comfortless is the sorrow of him who feels at once the pangs of guilt and the vexation of calamity which guilt has brought upon him?

"Consider, princess, what would have been your condition if the lady Pekuah had intreated to accompany you, and, being compelled to stay in the tents, had been carried away; or how would you have borne the thought if you had forced her into the pyramid and she had died before you in agonies of terror."

"Had either happened," said Nekayah, "I could not have endured life till now: I should have been tortured to madness by the remembrance of such cruelty, or must have pined away in abhorrence of myself."

"This at least," said Imlac, "is the present reward of virtuous conduct, that no unlucky consequence can oblige us to repent it."

CHAPTER XXXV

The Princess Languishes for Want of Pekuah

Nekayah, being thus reconciled to herself, found that no evil is insupportable but that which is accompanied with consciousness of wrong. She was, from that time, delivered from the violence of tempestuous sorrow and sunk into silent pensiveness and gloomy tranquillity. She sat from morning to evening recollecting all that had been done or said by her Pekuah, treasured up with care every trifle on which Pekuah had set an accidental value and which might recall to mind any little incident or careless conversation. The sentiments of her whom she now expected to see no more were treasured in her memory as rules of life, and she deliberated to no other end than to conjecture on any occasion what would have been the opinion and counsel of Pekuah.

The women by whom she was attended knew nothing of her real condition, and therefore she could not talk to them but with caution and reserve. She began to remit her curiosity, having no great care to collect notions which she had no convenience of uttering. Rasselas endeavoured first to comfort and afterwards to divert her; he hired musicians, to whom she seemed to listen but did not hear them, and procured masters to instruct her in various arts, whose lectures, when they visited her again, were again to be repeated. She had lost her taste of pleasure and her ambition of excellence. And her mind, though forced into short excursions, always recurred to the image of her friend.

Imlac was every morning earnestly enjoined [1] to renew his enquiries, and was asked every night whether he had yet heard of Pekuah, till not being able to return the princess the answer that she desired, he was less and less willing to come into her presence. She observed his backwardness, and commanded him to attend her. "You are not," said she, "to confound impatience with resentment, or to suppose that I charge you with negligence because I repine at your unsuccessfulness. I do not much wonder at your absence; I know that the unhappy are never pleasing and that all naturally avoid the contagion of misery. To hear complaints is wearisome alike to the wretched and the happy; for who would cloud by adventitious grief the short gleams of gaiety which life allows us? or who that is struggling under his own evils will add to them the miseries of another?

"The time is at hand when none shall be disturbed any longer by the sighs of Nekayah: my search after happiness is now at an end. I am resolved to retire from the world with all its flatteries and deceits, and will hide myself in solitude, without any other care than to compose my thoughts and regulate my hours by a constant succession of innocent occupations, till, with a mind purified from all earthly desires, I shall enter into that state to which all are hastening and in which I hope again to enjoy the friendship of Pekuah."

"Do not entangle your mind," said Imlac, "by irrevocable determinations, nor increase the burden of life by a voluntary accumulation of misery: the weariness of retirement will continue or increase when the loss of Pekuah

[1] enjoined "to direct; to order. . . . It is more authoritative than *direct,* and less imperious than *command*" (*Dictionary*)

is forgotten. That you have been deprived of one pleasure is no very good reason for rejection of the rest."

"Since Pekuah was taken from me," said the princess, "I have no pleasure to reject or to retain. She that has no one to love or trust has little to hope. She wants the radical principle of happiness. We may, perhaps, allow that what satisfaction this world can afford must arise from the conjunction of wealth, knowledge and goodness: wealth is nothing but as it is bestowed, and knowledge nothing but as it is communicated: they must therefore be imparted to others, and to whom could I now delight to impart them? Goodness affords the only comfort which can be enjoyed without a partner, and goodness may be practised in retirement."

"How far solitude may admit goodness or advance it, I shall not," replied Imlac, "dispute at present. Remember the confession of the pious hermit. You will wish to return into the world when the image of your companion has left your thoughts." "That time," said Nekayah, "will never come. The generous frankness, the modest obsequiousness,[2] and the faithful secrecy of my dear Pekuah will always be more missed, as I shall live longer to see vice and folly."

"The state of a mind oppressed with a sudden calamity," said Imlac, "is like that of the fabulous inhabitants of the new created earth, who, when the first night came upon them, supposed that day never would return. When the clouds of sorrow gather over us, we see nothing beyond them, nor can imagine how they will be dispelled: yet a new day succeeded to the night, and sorrow is never long without a dawn of ease. But they who restrain themselves from receiving comfort do as the savages would have done had they put out their eyes when it was dark. Our minds, like our bodies, are in continual flux; something is hourly lost, and something acquired. To lose much at once is inconvenient to either, but while the vital powers remain uninjured, nature will find the means of reparation. Distance has the same effect on the mind as on the eye, and while we glide along the stream of time, whatever we leave behind us is always lessening, and that which we approach increasing in magnitude. Do not suffer life to

---

[2] obsequiousness "obedience; compliance" (*Dictionary*)

stagnate; it will grow muddy for want of motion: commit yourself again to the current of the world; Pekuah will vanish by degrees; you will meet in your way some other favourite, or learn to diffuse yourself in general conversation."

"At least," said the prince, "do not despair before all remedies have been tried: the enquiry after the unfortunate lady is still continued, and shall be carried on with yet greater diligence, on condition that you will promise to wait a year for the event without any unalterable resolution."

Nekayah thought this a reasonable demand and made the promise to her brother, who had been advised by Imlac to require it. Imlac had, indeed, no great hope of regaining Pekuah, but he supposed that if he could secure the interval of a year the princess would be then in no danger of a cloister.

CHAPTER XXXVI

PEKUAH IS STILL REMEMBERED. THE PROGRESS OF SORROW

Nekayah, seeing that nothing was omitted for the recovery of her favourite, and having, by her promise, set her intention of retirement at a distance, began imperceptibly to return to common cares and common pleasures. She rejoiced without her own consent at the suspension of her sorrows, and sometimes caught herself with indignation in the act of turning away her mind from the remembrance of her whom yet she resolved never to forget.

She then appointed a certain hour of the day for meditation on the merits and fondness of Pekuah, and for some weeks retired constantly at the time fixed, and returned with her eyes swollen and her countenance clouded. By degrees she grew less scrupulous, and suffered any important and pressing avocation[1] to delay the tribute of daily tears. She then yielded to less occasions; sometimes forgot what she was indeed afraid to remember, and, at

[1] avocation "the business that calls" (*Dictionary*)

last, wholly released herself from the duty of periodical affliction.

Her real love of Pekuah was yet not diminished. A thousand occurrences brought her back to memory, and a thousand wants, which nothing but the confidence of friendship can supply, made her frequently regretted. She therefore solicited Imlac never to desist from enquiry and to leave no art of intelligence untried, that, at least, she might have the comfort of knowing that she did not suffer by negligence or sluggishness. "Yet what," said she, "is to be expected from our pursuit of happiness, when we find the state of life to be such that happiness itself is the cause of misery? Why should we endeavour to attain that of which the possession cannot be secured? I shall henceforward fear to yield my heart to excellence, however bright, or to fondness, however tender, lest I should lose again what I have lost in Pekuah."

CHAPTER XXXVII

The Princess Hears News of Pekuah

In seven months, one of the messengers, who had been sent away upon the day when the promise was drawn from the princess, returned, after many unsuccessful rambles, from the borders of Nubia,[1] with an account that Pekuah was in the hands of an Arab chief, who possessed a castle or fortress on the extremity of Egypt. The Arab, whose revenue was plunder, was willing to restore her, with her two attendants, for two hundred ounces of gold.

The price was no subject of debate. The princess was in ecstasies when she heard that her favourite was alive and might so cheaply be ransomed. She could not think of delaying for a moment Pekuah's happiness or her own, but entreated her brother to send back the messenger with the sum required. Imlac, being consulted, was not very confident of the veracity of the relater, and was still more doubtful of the Arab's faith, who might, if he were too

[1] Nubia region in the Nile valley, now a part of Egypt and the Sudan

liberally trusted, detain at once the money and the captives. He thought it dangerous to put themselves in the power of the Arab by going into his district, and could not expect that the Rover[2] would so much expose himself as to come into the lower country, where he might be seized by the forces of the Bassa.

It is difficult to negotiate where neither will trust. But Imlac, after some deliberation, directed the messenger to propose that Pekuah should be conducted by ten horsemen to the monastery of St. Antony,[3] which is situated in the deserts of Upper-Egypt, where she should be met by the same number, and her ransom should be paid.

That no time might be lost, as they expected that the proposal would not be refused, they immediately began their journey to the monastery; and, when they arrived, Imlac went forward with the former messenger to the Arab's fortress. Rasselas was desirous to go with them, but neither his sister nor Imlac would consent. The Arab, according to the custom of his nation, observed the laws of hospitality with great exactness to those who put themselves into his power, and, in a few days, brought Pekuah with her maids, by easy journeys, to their place appointed, where receiving the stipulated price, he restored her with great respect to liberty and her friends, and undertook to conduct them back towards Cairo beyond all danger of robbery or violence.

The princess and her favourite embraced each other with transport too violent to be expressed, and went out together to pour the tears of tenderness in secret and exchange professions of kindness and gratitude. After a few hours they returned into the refectory of the convent, where, in the presence of the prior and his brethren, the prince required of Pekuah the history of her adventures.

[2] **Rover** "a robber" (*Dictionary*)
[3] **St. Antony** references to the order of monks founded by St. Anthony appear in several early accounts of Egypt and Abyssinia

CHAPTER XXXVIII

The Adventures of the Lady Pekuah

"At what time and in what manner, I was forced away," said Pekuah, "your servants have told you. The suddenness of the event struck me with surprise, and I was at first rather stupefied than agitated with any passion of either fear or sorrow. My confusion was increased by the speed and tumult of our flight while we were followed by the Turks, who, as it seemed, soon despaired to overtake us, or were afraid of those whom they made a show of menacing.

"When the Arabs saw themselves out of danger they slackened their course, and, as I was less harassed by external violence, I began to feel more uneasiness in my mind. After some time we stopped near a spring shaded with trees in a pleasant meadow, where we were set upon the ground, and offered such refreshments as our masters were partaking. I was suffered to sit with my maids apart from the rest, and none attempted to comfort or insult us. Here I first began to feel the full weight of my misery. The girls sat weeping in silence, and from time to time looked on me for succour. I knew not to what condition we were doomed, nor could conjecture where would be the place of our captivity, or whence to draw any hope of deliverance. I was in the hands of robbers and savages, and had no reason to suppose that their pity was more than their justice, or that they would forbear the gratification of any ardour of desire or caprice of cruelty. I, however, kissed my maids and endeavoured to pacify them by remarking that we were yet treated with decency and that, since we were now carried beyond pursuit, there was no danger of violence to our lives.

"When we were to be set again on horseback, my maids clung round me and refused to be parted, but I commanded them not to irritate those who had us in their power. We travelled the remaining part of the day through an unfrequented and pathless country, and came by moonlight to the side of a hill, where the rest of the troop was stationed. Their tents were pitched and their fires kindled, and our chief was welcomed as a man much beloved by his dependants.

"We were received into a large tent, where we found women who had attended their husbands in the expedition. They set before us the supper which they had provided, and I eat it rather to encourage my maids than to comply with any appetite of my own. When the meat was taken away they spread the carpets for repose. I was weary, and hoped to find in sleep that remission of distress which nature seldom denies. Ordering myself therefore to be undressed, I observed that the women looked very earnestly upon me, not expecting, I suppose, to see me so submissively attended. When my upper vest was taken off, they were apparently struck with the splendour of my clothes, and one of them timorously laid her hand upon the embroidery. She then went out, and, in a short time, came back with another woman, who seemed to be of higher rank and greater authority. She did, at her entrance, the usual act of reverence,[1] and, taking me by the hand, placed me in a smaller tent, spread with finer carpets, where I spent the night quietly with my maids.

"In the morning, as I was sitting on the grass, the chief of the troop came towards me. I rose up to receive him, and he bowed with great respect. "Illustrious lady," said he, "my fortune is better than I had presumed to hope; I am told by my women that I have a princess in my camp." "Sir," answered I, "your women have deceived themselves and you; I am not a princess, but an unhappy stranger who intended soon to have left this country, in which I am now to be imprisoned forever." "Whoever, or whencesoever, you are," returned the Arab, "your dress, and that of your servants, show your rank to be high and your wealth to be great. Why should you, who can so easily procure your ransom, think yourself in danger of perpetual captivity? The purpose of my incursions is to increase my riches, or more properly to gather tribute. The sons of Ishmael [2] are the natural and hereditary lords

[1] reverence "act of obeisance; bow; courtesy" (*Dictionary*)

[2] Ishmael the Arabs claim to be the descendants of Ishmael, son of Abraham and Hagar (Genesis 16:15)

of this part of the continent, which is usurped by late invaders and low-born tyrants, from whom we are compelled to take by the sword what is denied to justice. The violence of war admits no distinction; the lance that is lifted at guilt and power will sometimes fall on innocence and gentleness."

"How little," said I, "did I expect that yesterday it should have fallen upon me."

"Misfortunes," answered the Arab, "should always be expected. If the eye of hostility could learn reverence or pity, excellence like yours had been exempt from injury. But the angels of affliction spread their toils alike for the virtuous and the wicked, for the mighty and the mean. Do not be disconsolate; I am not one of the lawless and cruel rovers of the desert; I know the rules of civil [3] life: I will fix your ransom, give a passport to your messenger, and perform my stipulation with nice punctuality." [4]

"You will easily believe that I was pleased with his courtesy; and finding that his predominant passion was desire of money, I began now to think my danger less, for I knew that no sum would be thought too great for the release of Pekuah. I told him that he should have no reason to charge me with ingratitude if I was used with kindness, and that any ransom which could be expected for a maid of common rank would be paid, but that he must not persist to rate me as a princess. He said he would consider what he should demand, and then, smiling, bowed and retired.

"Soon after the women came about me, each contending to be more officious than the other, and my maids themselves were served with reverence. We travelled onward by short journeys. On the fourth day the chief told me that my ransom must be two hundred ounces of gold, which I not only promised him but told him that I would add fifty more if I and my maids were honourably treated.

"I never knew the power of gold before. From that time I was the leader of the troop. The march of every day was longer or shorter as I commanded, and the tents were pitched where I chose to rest. We now had camels and

[3] **civil** "civilized; gentle; well bred" (*Dictionary*)
[4] **punctuality** "nicety; scrupulous exactness" (*Dictionary*)

other conveniences for travel, my own women were always at my side, and I amused myself with observing the manners of the vagrant nations, and with viewing remains of ancient edifices with which these deserted countries appear to have been, in some distant age, lavishly embellished.

"The chief of the band was a man far from illiterate: he was able to travel by the stars or the compass, and had marked in his erratic expeditions such places as are most worthy the notice of a passenger. He observed to me that buildings are always best preserved in places little frequented and difficult of access: for, when once a country declines from its primitive splendour, the more inhabitants are left, the quicker ruin will be made. Walls supply stones more easily than quarries, and palaces and temples will be demolished to make stables of granite and cottages of porphyry.

CHAPTER XXXIX

The Adventures of Pekuah Continued

"We wandered about in this manner for some weeks, whether, as our chief pretended, for my gratification, or, as I rather suspected, for some convenience of his own. I endeavoured to appear contented where sullenness and resentment would have been of no use, and that endeavour conduced much to the calmness of my mind; but my heart was always with Nekayah, and the troubles of the night much overbalanced the amusements of the day. My women, who threw all their cares upon their mistress, set their minds at ease from the time when they saw me treated with respect, and gave themselves up to the incidental alleviations of our fatigue without solicitude or sorrow. I was pleased with their pleasure and animated with their confidence. My condition had lost much of its terror, since I found that the Arab ranged the country merely to get riches. Avarice is an uniform and tractable vice; other intellectual distempers are different in different constitutions of mind; that which sooths the pride of one will offend the pride of another; but to the favour of the covetous there is a ready way, bring money and nothing is denied.

"At last we came to the dwelling of our chief, a strong and spacious house built with stone in an island of the Nile, which lies, as I was told, under the tropic. 'Lady,' said the Arab, 'you shall rest after your journey a few weeks in this place, where you are to consider yourself as sovereign. My occupation is war: I have therefore chosen this obscure residence, from which I can issue unexpected and to which I can retire unpursued. You may now repose in security: here are few pleasures, but here is no danger.' He then led me into the inner apartments, and seating me on the richest couch, bowed to the ground. His women, who considered me as a rival, looked on me with malignity; but being soon informed that I was a great lady detained only for my ransom, they began to vie with each other in obsequiousness and reverence.

"Being again comforted with new assurances of speedy liberty, I was for some days diverted from impatience by the novelty of the place. The turrets overlooked the country to a great distance, and afforded a view of many windings of the stream. In the day I wandered from one place to another as the course of the sun varied the splendour of the prospect, and saw many things which I had never seen before. The crocodiles and river-horses[1] are common in this unpeopled region, and I often looked upon them with terror, though I knew that they could not hurt me. For some time I expected to see mermaids and tritons, which, as Imlac has told me, the European travellers have stationed in the Nile, but no such beings ever appeared, and the Arab, when I enquired after them, laughed at my credulity.

"At night the Arab always attended me to a tower set apart for celestial observations, where he endeavoured to teach me the names and courses of the stars. I had no great inclination to this study, but an appearance of attention was necessary to please my instructor, who valued himself for his skill, and, in a little while, I found some employment requisite to beguile the tediousness of time, which was to be passed always amidst the same objects. I was weary of looking in the morning on things from which I

[1] **river-horses** hippopotamuses

had turned away weary in the evening: I therefore was at last willing to observe the stars rather than do nothing, but could not always compose my thoughts, and was very often thinking on Nekayah when others imagined me contemplating the sky. Soon after the Arab went upon another expedition, and then my only pleasure was to talk with my maids about the accident by which we were carried away, and the happiness that we should all enjoy at the end of our captivity."

"There were women in your Arab's fortress," said the princess, "why did you not make them your companions, enjoy their conversation, and partake their diversions? In a place where they found business or amusement, why should you alone sit corroded with idle melancholy? or why could not you bear for a few months that condition to which they were condemned for life?"

"The diversions of the women," answered Pekuah, "were only childish play, by which the mind accustomed to stronger operations could not be kept busy. I could do all which they delighted in doing by powers merely sensitive,[2] while my intellectual faculties were flown to Cairo. They ran from room to room as a bird hops from wire to wire in his cage. They danced for the sake of motion, as lambs frisk in a meadow. One sometimes pretended to be hurt that the rest might be alarmed, or hid herself that another might seek her. Part of their time passed in watching the progress of light bodies that floated on the river, and part in marking the various forms into which clouds broke in the sky.

"Their business was only needlework, in which I and my maids sometimes helped them; but you know that the mind will easily straggle from the fingers, nor will you suspect that captivity and absence from Nekayah could receive solace from silken flowers.

"Nor was much satisfaction to be hoped from their conversation: for of what could they be expected to talk? They had seen nothing; for they had lived from early youth in that narrow spot: of what they had not seen they could have no knowledge, for they could not read. They had no

---

[2] sensitive "having sense or perception, but not reason" (*Dictionary*)

ideas but of the few things that were within their view, and had hardly names for anything but their clothes and their food. As I bore a superior character, I was often called to terminate their quarrels, which I decided as equitably as I could. If it could have amused me to hear the complaints of each against the rest, I might have been often detained by long stories, but the motives of their animosity were so small that I could not listen without intercepting[3] the tale."

"How," said Rasselas, "can the Arab, whom you represented as a man of more than common accomplishments, take any pleasure in his seraglio,[4] when it is filled only with women like these. Are they exquisitely beautiful?"

"They do not," said Pekuah, "want that unaffecting[5] and ignoble beauty which may subsist without sprightliness or sublimity, without energy of thought or dignity of virtue. But to a man like the Arab such beauty was only a flower casually plucked and carelessly thrown away. Whatever pleasures he might find among them, they were not those of friendship or society. When they were playing about him he looked on them with inattentive superiority: when they vied for his regard he sometimes turned away disgusted. As they had no knowledge, their talk could take nothing from the tediousness of life: as they had no choice, their fondness or appearance of fondness excited in him neither pride nor gratitude; he was not exalted in his own esteem by the smiles of a woman who saw no other man, nor was much obliged [6] by that regard of which he could never know the sincerity, and which he might often perceive to be exerted not so much to delight him as to pain a rival. That which he gave, and they received, as love was only a careless distribution of superfluous time, such love as man can bestow upon that which he despises, such as has neither hope nor fear, neither joy nor sorrow."

"You have reason, lady, to think yourself happy," said

[3] intercepting "to cut off; to stop from being communicated" (*Dictionary*)
[4] seraglio "a house of women kept for debauchery" (*Dictionary*)
[5] unaffecting "not moving the passions" (*Dictionary*)
[6] obliged "to please; to gratify" (*Dictionary*)

Imlac, "that you have been thus easily dismissed. How could a mind, hungry for knowledge, be willing, in an intellectual famine, to lose such a banquet as Pekuah's conversation?"

"I am inclined to believe," answered Pekuah, "that he was for some time in suspense; for, notwithstanding his promise, whenever I proposed to dispatch a messenger to Cairo, he found some excuse for delay. While I was detained in his house he made many incursions into the neighbouring countries, and, perhaps, he would have refused to discharge me had his plunder been equal to his wishes. He returned always courteous, related his adventures, delighted to hear my observations, and endeavoured to advance my acquaintance with the stars. When I importuned him to send away my letters, he soothed me with professions of honour and sincerity; and, when I could be no longer decently denied, put his troop again in motion, and left me to govern in his absence. I was much afflicted by this studied procrastination, and was sometimes afraid that I should be forgotten; that you would leave Cairo, and I must end my days in an island of the Nile.

"I grew at last hopeless and dejected, and cared so little to entertain him that he for a while more frequently talked with my maids. That he should fall in love with them, or with me, might have been equally fatal, and I was not much pleased with the growing friendship. My anxiety was not long; for as I recovered some degrees of cheerfulness, he returned to me, and I could not forbear to despise my former uneasiness.

"He still delayed to send for my ransom, and would, perhaps, never have determined, had not your agent found his way to him. The gold which he would not fetch he could not reject when it was offered. He hastened to prepare for our journey hither, like a man delivered from the pain of an intestine conflict. I took leave of my companions in the house, who dismissed me with cold indifference."

Nekayah, having heard her favourite's relation, rose and embraced her, and Rasselas gave her an hundred ounces of gold, which she presented to the Arab for the fifty that were promised.

CHAPTER XL

THE HISTORY OF A MAN OF LEARNING

They returned to Cairo, and were so well pleased at finding themselves together that none of them went much abroad. The prince began to love learning, and one day declared to Imlac that he intended to devote himself to science,[1] and pass the rest of his days in literary solitude.

"Before you make your final choice," answered Imlac, "you ought to examine its hazards, and converse with some of those who are grown old in the company of themselves. I have just left the observatory of one of the most learned astronomers[2] in the world, who has spent forty years in unwearied attention to the motions and appearances of the celestial bodies, and has drawn out his soul in endless calculations. He admits a few friends once a month to hear his deductions and enjoy his discoveries. I was introduced as a man of knowledge worthy of his notice. Men of various ideas and fluent conversation are commonly welcome to those whose thoughts have been long fixed upon a single point, and who find the images of other things stealing away. I delighted him with my remarks, he smiled at the narrative of my travels, and was glad to forget the constellations and descend for a moment into the lower world.

"On the next day of vacation I renewed my visit, and was so fortunate as to please him again. He relaxed from that time the severity of his rule, and permitted me to enter at my own choice. I found him always busy, and always glad to be relieved. As each knew much which the other was desirous of learning, we exchanged our notions with great delight. I perceived that I had every day more

[1] science "knowledge" (*Dictionary*)
[2] astronomers in the *Dictionary* under *astronomy*, Johnson cites a quotation asserting that "from Egypt" astronomy "travelled into Greece" and that the science was later "revived by the Ptolemys, kings of Egypt"

of his confidence, and always found new cause of admiration in the profundity of his mind. His comprehension is vast, his memory capacious and retentive, his discourse is methodical, and his expression clear.

"His integrity and benevolence are equal to his learning. His deepest researches and most favourite studies are willingly interrupted for any opportunity of doing good by his counsel or his riches. To his closest[a] retreat, at his most busy moments, all are admitted that want his assistance: 'For though I exclude idleness and pleasure, I will never, says he, bar my doors against charity. To man is permitted the contemplation of the skies, but the practice of virtue is commanded.'

"Surely," said the princess, "this man is happy."

"I visited him," said Imlac, "with more and more frequency, and was every time more enamoured of his conversation: he was sublime without haughtiness, courteous without formality, and communicative without ostentation. I was at first, great princess, of your opinion, thought him the happiest of mankind, and often congratulated him on the blessing that he enjoyed. He seemed to hear nothing with indifference but the praises of his condition, to which he always returned a general answer, and diverted the conversation to some other topic.

"Amidst this willingness to be pleased, and labour to please, I had quickly reason to imagine that some painful sentiment pressed upon his mind. He often looked up earnestly towards the sun, and let his voice fall in the midst of his discourse. He would sometimes, when we were alone, gaze upon me in silence with the air of a man who longed to speak what he was yet resolved to suppress. He would often send for me with vehement injunctions of haste, though, when I came to him, he had nothing extraordinary to say. And sometimes, when I was leaving him, would call me back, pause a few moments and then dismiss me."

[a] closest "secret; private" (*Dictionary*)

CHAPTER XLI

THE ASTRONOMER DISCOVERS THE CAUSE OF HIS UNEASINESS

"At last the time came when the secret burst his reserve. We were sitting together last night in the turret of his house, watching the emersion[1] of a satellite of Jupiter. A sudden tempest clouded the sky and disappointed our observation. We sat a while silent in the dark, and then he addressed himself to me in these words: 'Imlac, I have long considered thy friendship as the greatest blessing of my life. Integrity without knowledge is weak and useless, and knowledge without integrity is dangerous and dreadful. I have found in thee all the qualities requisite for trust, benevolence, experience, and fortitude. I have long discharged an office which I must soon quit at the call of nature, and shall rejoice in the hour of imbecility and pain to devolve it upon thee.'

"I thought myself honoured by this testimony, and protested that whatever could conduce to his happiness would add likewise to mine."

"'Hear, Imlac, what thou wilt not without difficulty credit. I have possessed for five years the regulation of weather and the distribution of the seasons: the sun has listened to my dictates, and passed from tropic to tropic by my direction; the clouds, at my call, have poured their waters, and the Nile has overflowed at my command; I have restrained the rage of the dog-star,[2] and mitigated the fervours of the crab.[3] The winds alone, of all the elemental powers, have hitherto refused my authority, and multitudes have perished by equinoctial tempests which I

[1] emersion "the time when a star, having been obscured by its too near approach to the sun, appears again" (*Dictionary*)

[2] dog-star "the star [Sirius] which gives the name to the dog-days," "vulgarly reputed unwholesome" (*Dictionary*)

[3] crab "the sign in the zodiack" (*Dictionary*) and the constellation Cancer

found myself unable to prohibit or restrain. I have administered this great office with exact justice, and made to the different nations of the earth an impartial dividend of rain and sunshine. What must have been the misery of half the globe if I had limited the clouds to particular regions, or confined the sun to either side of the equator?' "

CHAPTER XLII

The Opinion of the Astronomer is Explained and Justified

"I suppose he discovered in me, through the obscurity of the room, some tokens of amazement and doubt, for, after a short pause, he proceeded thus:

" 'Not to be easily credited will neither surprise nor offend me; for I am, probably, the first of human beings to whom this trust has been imparted. Nor do I know whether to deem this distinction a reward or punishment; since I have possessed it I have been far less happy than before, and nothing but the consciousness of good intention could have enabled me to support the weariness of unremitted vigilance.'

"How long, Sir," said I, "has this great office been in your hands?"

" 'About ten years ago,' " said he, " 'my daily observations of the changes of the sky led me to consider whether, if I had the power of the seasons, I could confer greater plenty upon the inhabitants of the earth. This contemplation fastened on my mind, and I sat days and nights in imaginary dominion, pouring upon this country and that the showers of fertility, and seconding every fall of rain with a due proportion of sunshine. I had yet only the will to do good, and did not imagine that I should ever have the power.

" 'One day as I was looking on the fields withering with heat, I felt in my mind a sudden wish that I could send rain on the southern mountains and raise the Nile to an inundation. In the hurry of my imagination I commanded rain to fall, and, by comparing the time of my command with that of the inundation, I found that the clouds had listened to my lips.'

"Might not some other cause," said I, "produce this concurrence? the Nile does not always rise on the same day." [1]

" 'Do not believe,' " said he with impatience, " 'that such objections could escape me: I reasoned long against my own conviction, and laboured against truth with the utmost obstinacy. I sometimes suspected myself of madness, and should not have dared to impart this secret but to a man like you, capable of distinguishing the wonderful from the impossible, and the incredible from the false.'

"Why, Sir," said I, "do you call that incredible which you know, or think you know, to be true?"

" 'Because,' " said he, " 'I cannot prove it by any external evidence; and I know too well the laws of demonstration to think that my conviction ought to influence another, who cannot, like me, be conscious of its force. I, therefore, shall not attempt to gain credit by disputation. It is sufficient that I feel this power, that I have long possessed, and every day exerted it. But the life of man is short, the infirmities of age increase upon me, and the time will soon come when the regulator of the year must mingle with the dust. The care of appointing a successor has long disturbed me; the night and the day have been spent in comparisons of all the characters which have come to my knowledge, and I have yet found none so worthy as thyself.' "

CHAPTER XLIII

The Astronomer Leaves Imlac His Directions

" 'Hear therefore, what I shall impart with attention such as the welfare of a world requires. If the task of a king be considered as difficult, who has the care only of a few millions, to whom he cannot do much good or harm, what

[1] **same day** according to at least one seventeenth-century writer, the Egyptians believed that the annual overflow of the Nile began on the same day each year

must be the anxiety of him on whom depends the action of the elements, and the great gifts of light and heat!—Hear me therefore with attention.

"'I have diligently considered the position of the earth and sun, and formed innumerable schemes in which I changed their situation. I have sometimes turned aside the axis of the earth, and sometimes varied the ecliptic of the sun: but I have found it impossible to make a disposition by which the world may be advantaged; what one region gains, another loses by any imaginable alteration, even without considering the distant parts of the solar system with which we are unacquainted. Do not, therefore, in thy administration of the year indulge thy pride by innovation; do not please thyself with thinking that thou canst make thyself renowned to all future ages by disordering the seasons. The memory of mischief is no desirable fame. Much less will it become thee to let kindness or interest prevail. Never rob other countries of rain to pour it on thine own. For us the Nile is sufficient.'

"I promised that when I possessed the power, I would use it with inflexible integrity, and he dismissed me, pressing my hand." "'My heart,'" said he, "'will be now at rest, and my benevolence will no more destroy my quiet: I have found a man of wisdom and virtue, to whom I can cheerfully bequeath the inheritance of the sun.'"

The prince heard this narration with very serious regard, but the princess smiled, and Pekuah convulsed herself with laughter. "Ladies," said Imlac, "to mock the heaviest of human afflictions is neither charitable nor wise. Few can attain this man's knowledge, and few practise his virtues; but all may suffer his calamity. Of the uncertainties of our present state, the most dreadful and alarming is the uncertain continuance of reason."

The princess was recollected,[1] and the favourite was abashed. Rasselas, more deeply affected, enquired of Imlac whether he thought such maladies of the mind frequent, and how they were contracted.

[1] recollected "to recover reason" (*Dictionary*)

CHAPTER XLIV

THE DANGEROUS PREVALENCE OF IMAGINATION[1]

"Disorders of intellect," answered Imlac, "happen much more often than superficial observers will easily believe. Perhaps, if we speak with rigorous exactness, no human mind is in its right state. There is no man whose imagination does not sometimes predominate over his reason, who can regulate his attention wholly by his will, and whose ideas will come and go at his command. No man will be found in whose mind airy[2] notions do not sometimes tyrannize, and force him to hope or fear beyond the limits of sober probability. All power of fancy over reason is a degree of insanity; but while this power is such as we can control and repress, it is not visible to others nor considered as any depravation of the mental faculties: it is not pronounced madness but when it comes[3] ungovernable, and apparently influences speech or action.

"To indulge the power of fiction, and send imagination out upon the wing, is often the sport of those who delight too much in silent speculation. When we are alone we are not always busy; the labour of excogitation is too violent to last long; the ardour of enquiry will sometimes give way to idleness or satiety. He who has nothing external that can divert him, must find pleasure in his own thoughts, and must conceive himself what he is not; for who is pleased with what he is? He then expatiates[4] in boundless futurity, and culls from all imaginable conditions that which for the present moment he should most desire, amuses his desires with impossible enjoyments, and confers upon his pride unattainable dominion. The mind dances from scene to

[1] Imlac's remarks in this chapter exemplify a common seventeenth- and eighteenth-century attitude toward the imagination
[2] airy "without reality; without any steady foundation in truth or nature" (*Dictionary*)
[3] comes "to become" (*Dictionary*)
[4] expatiates "to range at large" (*Dictionary*)

scene, unites all pleasures in all combinations, and riots in delights which nature and fortune, with all their bounty, cannot bestow.

"In time some particular train of ideas fixes the attention, all other intellectual gratifications are rejected, the mind, in weariness or leisure, recurs constantly to the favourite conception, and feasts on the luscious[5] falsehood whenever she is offended with the bitterness of truth. By degrees the reign of fancy is confirmed; she grows first imperious and in time despotic. Then fictions begin to operate as realities, false opinions[6] fasten upon the mind, and life passes in dreams of rapture or of anguish.

"This, Sir, is one of the dangers of solitude, which the hermit has confessed not always to promote goodness, and the astronomer's misery has proved to be not always propitious to wisdom."

"I will no more," said the favourite, "imagine myself the queen of Abyssinia. I have often spent the hours which the princess gave to my own disposal in adjusting ceremonies and regulating the court; I have repressed the pride of the powerful, and granted the petitions of the poor; I have built new palaces in more-happy situations, planted groves upon the tops of mountains, and have exulted in the beneficence of royalty, till, when the princess entered, I had almost forgotten to bow down before her."

"And I," said the princess, "will not allow myself any more to play the shepherdess in my waking dreams. I have often soothed my thoughts with the quiet and innocence of pastoral employments, till I have in my chamber heard the winds whistle and the sheep bleat; sometimes freed the lamb entangled in the thicket, and sometimes with my crook encountered the wolf. I have a dress like that of the village maids, which I put on to help my imagination, and a pipe on which I play softly, and suppose myself followed by my flocks."

"I will confess," said the prince, "an indulgence of fantastic delight more dangerous than yours. I have frequently endeavoured to image the possibility of a perfect

---

[5] luscious "pleasing; delightful" (*Dictionary*)

[6] opinions "persuasion of the mind, without proof or certain knowledge" (*Dictionary*)

government, by which all wrong should be restrained, all vice reformed, and all the subjects preserved in tranquility and innocence. This thought produced innumerable schemes of reformation, and dictated many useful regulations and salutary edicts. This has been the sport and sometimes the labour of my solitude; and I start when I think with how little anguish I once supposed the death of my father and my brothers."

"Such," says Imlac, "are the effects of visionary schemes: when we first form them we know them to be absurd, but familiarize them by degrees, and in time lose sight of their folly."

CHAPTER XLV

THEY DISCOURSE WITH AN OLD MAN

The evening was now far past, and they rose to return home. As they walked along the bank of the Nile, delighted with the beams of the moon quivering on the water, they saw at a small distance an old man whom the prince had often heard in the assembly of the sages. "Yonder," said he, "is one whose years have calmed his passions but not clouded his reason: let us close the disquisitions of the night by enquiring what are his sentiments of his own state, that we may know whether youth alone is to struggle with vexation, and whether any better hope remains for the latter part of life."

Here the sage approached and saluted them. They invited him to join their walk, and prattled[1] a while as acquaintance that had unexpectedly met one another. The old man was cheerful and talkative, and the way seemed short in his company. He was pleased to find himself not disregarded, accompanied them to their house, and, at the prince's request, entered with them. They placed him in the seat of honour, and set wine and conserves before him.

"Sir," said the princess, "an evening walk must give to a man of learning, like you, pleasures which ignorance

[1] **prattled** "to talk lightly; to chatter" (*Dictionary*)

and youth can hardly conceive. You know the qualities and the causes of all that you behold, the laws by which the river flows, the periods in which the planets perform their revolutions. Everything must supply you with contemplation, and renew the consciousness of your own dignity." [2]

"Lady," answered he, "let the gay and the vigorous expect pleasure in their excursions, it is enough that age can obtain ease. To me the world has lost its novelty: I look round and see what I remember to have seen in happier days. I rest against a tree, and consider that in the same shade I once disputed upon the annual overflow of the Nile with a friend who is now silent in the grave. I cast my eyes upwards, fix them on the changing moon, and think with pain on the vicissitudes of life. I have ceased to take much delight in physical truth; for what have I to do with those things which I am soon to leave?"

"You may at least recreate yourself," said Imlac, "with the recollection of an honourable and useful life, and enjoy the praise which all agree to give you."

"Praise," said the sage, with a sigh, "is to an old man an empty sound. I have neither mother to be delighted with the reputation of her son, nor wife to partake the honours of her husband. I have outlived my friends and my rivals. Nothing is now of much importance; for I cannot extend my interest beyond myself. Youth is delighted with applause, because it is considered as the earnest of some future good, and because the prospect of life is far extended: but to me, who am now declining to decrepitude,[3] there is little to be feared from the malevolence of men, and yet less to be hoped from their affection or esteem. Something they may yet take away, but they can give me nothing. Riches would now be useless, and high employment would be pain. My retrospect of life recalls to my view many opportunities of good neglected, much time squandered upon trifles, and more lost in idleness and vacancy. I leave many great designs unattempted, and

[2] dignity "advancement; . . . high place [in knowledge]" (*Dictionary*)

[3] decrepitude "the last stage of decay; the last effects of old age" (*Dictionary*)

many great attempts unfinished. My mind is burdened with no heavy crime, and therefore I compose myself to tranquility; endeavour to abstract my thoughts from hopes and cares which, though reason knows them to be vain, still try to keep their old possession of the heart; expect, with serene humility, that hour which nature cannot long delay; and hope to possess in a better state that happiness which here I could not find, and that virtue which here I have not attained."

He rose and went away, leaving his audience not much elated with the hope of long life. The prince consoled himself with remarking that it was not reasonable to be disappointed by this account; for age had never been considered as the season of felicity, and, if it was possible to be easy in decline and weakness, it was likely that the days of vigour and alacrity might be happy; that the noon of life might be bright, if the evening could be calm.

The princess suspected that age was querulous and malignant, and delighted to repress the expectations of those who had newly entered the world. She had seen the possessors of estates look with envy on their heirs, and known many who enjoy pleasure no longer than they can confine it to themselves.

Pekuah conjected that the man was older than he appeared, and was willing to impute his complaints to delirious[4] dejection; or else supposed that he had been unfortunate and was therefore discontented: "For nothing," said she, "is more common than to call our own condition the condition of life."

Imlac, who had no desire to see them depressed, smiled at the comforts which they could so readily procure to themselves, and remembered that at the same age he was equally confident of unmingled prosperity, and equally fertile of consolatory expedients. He forbore to force upon them unwelcome knowledge, which time itself would too soon impress. The princess and her lady retired; the madness of the astronomer hung upon their minds, and they desired Imlac to enter upon his office and delay next morning the rising of the sun.

[4] **delirious** "doting" (*Dictionary*)

CHAPTER XLVI

The princess and Pekuah having talked in private of Imlac's astronomer, thought his character at once so amiable and so strange that they could not be satisfied without a nearer knowledge, and Imlac was requested to find the means of bringing them together.

This was somewhat difficult; the philosopher had never received any visits from women, though he lived in a city that had in it many Europeans who followed the manners of their own countries, and many from other parts of the world that lived there with European liberty. The ladies would not be refused, and several schemes were proposed for the accomplishment of their design. It was proposed to introduce them as strangers in distress, to whom the sage was always accessible; but, after some deliberation, it appeared that by this artifice no acquaintance could be formed, for their conversation would be short and they could not decently importune him often. "This," said Rasselas, "is true; but I have yet a stronger objection against the misrepresentation of your state. I have always considered it as treason against the great republic of human nature to make any man's virtues the means of deceiving him, whether on great or little occasions. All imposture weakens confidence and chills benevolence. When the sage finds that you are not what you seemed, he will feel the resentment natural to a man who, conscious of great abilities, discovers that he has been tricked by understandings meaner than his own, and, perhaps, the distrust which he can never afterwards wholly lay aside, may stop the voice of counsel, and close the hand of charity; and where will you find the power of restoring his benefactions to mankind or his peace to himself?"

To this no reply was attempted, and Imlac began to hope that their curiosity would subside; but next day Pekuah told him she had now found an honest pretence for a visit to the astronomer, for she would solicit permission to continue under him the studies in which she had been initiated by the Arab, and the princess might go with her either as a fellow-student or because a woman could not decently come alone. "I am afraid," said Imlac, "that he will be soon weary of your company: men advanced far in knowledge do not love to repeat the elements of their art, and I am not certain that even of the elements, as he will deliver them connected with inferences and mingled with reflections, you are a very capable auditress." "That," said Pekuah, "must be my care: I ask of you only to take me thither. My knowledge is, perhaps, more than you imagine it, and by concurring always with his opinions I shall make him think it greater than it is."

The astronomer, in pursuance of this resolution, was told that a foreign lady, travelling in search of knowledge, had heard of his reputation and was desirous to become his scholar. The uncommonness of the proposal raised at once his surprise and curiosity, and when, after a short deliberation, he consented to admit her, he could not stay[1] without impatience till the next day.

The ladies dressed themselves magnificently, and were attended by Imlac to the astronomer, who was pleased to see himself approached with respect by persons of so splendid an appearance. In the exchange of the first civilities he was timorous and bashful; but when the talk became regular, he recollected his powers, and justified the character which Imlac had given. Enquiring of Pekuah what could have turned her inclination towards astronomy, he received from her a history of her adventure at the pyramid and of the time passed in the Arab's island. She told her tale with ease and elegance, and her conversation took possession of his heart. The discourse was then turned to astronomy; Pekuah displayed what she knew: he looked upon her as a prodigy of genius, and intreated her not to desist from a study which she had so happily begun.

They came again and again, and were every time more welcome than before. The sage endeavoured to amuse them that they might prolong their visits, for he found his thoughts grow brighter in their company; the clouds of solicitude vanished by degrees as he forced himself to entertain them, and he grieved when he was left at their

[1] stay "to wait" (*Dictionary*)

departure to his old employment of regulating the seasons.

The princess and her favourite had now watched his lips for several months, and could not catch a single word from which they could judge whether he continued, or not, in the opinion of his preternatural commission. They often contrived[2] to bring him to an open declaration, but he easily eluded all their attacks, and on which side soever they pressed him escaped from them to some other topic.

As their familiarity increased they invited him often to the house of Imlac, where they distinguished him by extraordinary respect. He began gradually to delight in sublunary pleasures. He came early and departed late; laboured to recommend himself by assiduity and compliance;[3] excited their curiosity after new arts, that they might still want his assistance; and when they made any excursion of pleasure or enquiry, entreated to attend them.

By long experience of his integrity and wisdom, the prince and his sister were convinced that he might be trusted without danger; and, lest he should draw any false hopes from the civilities which he received, discovered to him their condition, with the motives of their journey, and required his opinion on the choice of life.

"Of the various conditions which the world spreads before you, which you shall prefer," said the sage, "I am not able to instruct you. I can only tell that I have chosen wrong. I have passed my time in study without experience; in the attainment of sciences which can, for the most part, be but remotely useful to mankind. I have purchased knowledge at the expence of all the common comforts of life: I have missed the endearing elegance of female friendship and the happy commerce of domestic tenderness. If I have obtained any prerogatives above other students, they have been accompanied with fear, disquiet, and scrupulosity; but even of these prerogatives, whatever they were, I have, since my thoughts have been diversified by more intercourse with the world, begun to question the reality. When I have been for a few days lost

[2] **contrived** "to form or design; to plan; to scheme; to complot" (*Dictionary*)

[3] **compliance** "a disposition to yield to others; complaisance" (*Dictionary*)

in pleasing dissipation, I am always tempted to think that my enquiries have ended in error and that I have suffered much, and suffered it in vain."

Imlac was delighted to find that the sage's understanding was breaking through its mists, and resolved to detain him from the planets till he should forget his task of ruling them, and reason should recover its original influence.

From this time the astronomer was received into familiar friendship and partook of all their projects and pleasures: his respect kept him attentive, and the activity of Rasselas did not leave much time unengaged. Something was always to be done; the day was spent in making observations which furnished talk for the evening, and the evening was closed with a scheme for the morrow.

The sage confessed to Imlac that since he had mingled in the gay tumults of life and divided his hours by a succession of amusements, he found the conviction of his authority over the skies fade gradually from his mind, and began to trust less to an opinion which he never could prove to others, and which he now found subject to variation from causes in which reason had no part. "If I am accidentally left alone for a few hours," said he, "my inveterate persuasion rushes upon my soul, and my thoughts are chained down by some irresistible violence, but they are soon disentangled by the prince's conversation, and instantaneously released at the entrance of Pekuah. I am like a man habitually afraid of spectres, who is set at ease by a lamp, and wonders at the dread which harassed him in the dark, yet, if his lamp be extinguished, feels again the terrors which he knows that when it is light he shall feel no more. But I am sometimes afraid lest I indulge my quiet by criminal negligence and voluntarily forget the great charge with which I am intrusted. If I favour myself in a known error, or am determined by my own ease in a doubtful question of this importance, how dreadful is my crime!"

"No disease of the imagination," answered Imlac, "is so difficult of cure as that which is complicated with the dread of guilt: fancy and conscience then act interchangeably upon us, and so often shift their places that the illusions of one are not distinguished from the dictates of the other. If fancy presents images not moral or religious, the mind drives them away when they give it pain, but when melancholic notions take the form of duty, they lay hold on the faculties without opposition because we are afraid to exclude or banish them. For this reason the super-stitious are often melancholy, and the melancholy almost always superstitious.

"But do not let the suggestions of timidity overpower your better reason: the danger of neglect can be but as the probability of the obligation, which, when you consider it with freedom, you find very little, and that little growing every day less. Open your heart to the influence of the light which, from time to time, breaks in upon you: when scruples[4] importune you which you in your lucid moments know to be vain, do not stand to parley, but fly to business or to Pekuah, and keep this thought always prevalent, that you are only one atom of the mass of humanity, and have neither such virtue nor vice as that you should be singled out for supernatural favours or afflictions."

CHAPTER XLVII

THE PRINCE ENTERS AND BRINGS A NEW TOPIC

"All this," said the astronomer, "I have often thought, but my reason has been so long subjugated by an uncontrollable and overwhelming idea that it durst not confide[1] in its own decisions. I now see how fatally I betrayed my quiet by suffering chimeras to prey upon me in secret; but melancholy shrinks from communication, and I never found a man before to whom I could impart my troubles, though I had been certain of relief. I rejoice to find my own sentiments confirmed by yours, who are not easily deceived and can have no motive or purpose to deceive. I hope that time and variety will dissipate the gloom that has so long surrounded me, and the latter part of my days will be spent in peace."

[4] **scruples** "doubt; difficulty of determination; perplexity: generally about minute things" (*Dictionary*)

[1] **confide** "to trust in; to put trust in" (*Dictionary*)

"Your learning and virtue," said Imlac, "may justly give you hopes."

Rasselas then entered with the princess and Pekuah, and enquired whether they had contrived any new diversion for the next day. "Such," said Nekayah, "is the state of life that none are happy but by the anticipation of change: the change itself is nothing; when we have made it, the next wish is to change again. The world is not yet exhausted; let me see something tomorrow which I never saw before."

"Variety," said Rasselas, "is so necessary to content that even the happy valley disgusted me by the recurrence of its luxuries; yet I could not forbear to reproach myself with impatience when I saw the monks of St. Anthony support without complaint a life, not of uniform delight, but uniform hardship."

"Those men," answered Imlac, "are less wretched in their silent convent than the Abyssinian princes in their prison of pleasure. Whatever is done by the monks is incited by an adequate and reasonable motive. Their labour supplies them with necessaries; it therefore cannot be omitted, and is certainly rewarded. Their devotion prepares them for another state and reminds them of its approach, while it fits them for it. Their time is regularly distributed; one duty succeeds another, so that they are not left open to the distraction of unguided choice nor lost in the shades of listless inactivity. There is a certain task to be performed at an appropriated hour; and their toils are cheerful because they consider them as acts of piety by which they are always advancing towards endless felicity."

"Do you think," said Nekayah, "that the monastic rule is a more holy and less imperfect state than any other? May not he equally hope for future happiness who converses[2] openly with mankind, who succours the distressed by his charity, instructs the ignorant by his learning, and contributes by his industry to the general system of life; even though he should omit some of the mortifications which are practised in the cloister, and allow himself such

[2] **converses** "to cohabit with; to hold intercourse with; to be a companion to: followed by *with*" (*Dictionary*)

harmless delights as his condition may place within his reach?"

"This," said Imlac, "is a question which has long divided the wise and perplexed the good. I am afraid to decide on either part. He that lives well in the world is better than he that lives well in a monastery. But, perhaps, every one is not able to stem the temptations of public life; and, if he cannot conquer, he may properly retreat. Some have little power to do good, and have likewise little strength to resist evil. Many are weary of their conflicts with adversity, and are willing to eject those passions which have long busied them in vain. And many are dismissed by age and diseases from the more laborious duties of society. In monasteries the weak and timorous may be happily sheltered, the weary may repose, and the penitent may meditate. Those retreats of prayer and contemplation have something so congenial to the mind of man that, perhaps, there is scarcely one that does not purpose to close his life in pious abstraction with a few associates serious as himself."

"Such," said Pekuah, "has often been my wish, and I have heard the princess declare that she should not willingly die in a crowd."

"The liberty of using harmless pleasures," proceeded Imlac, "will not be disputed; but it is still to be examined what pleasures are harmless. The evil of any pleasure that Nekayah can image is not in the act itself but in its consequences. Pleasure, in itself harmless, may become mischievous by endearing to us a state which we know to be transient and probatory,[3] and withdrawing our thoughts from that of which every hour brings us nearer to the beginning, and of which no length of time will bring us to the end. Mortification is not virtuous in itself nor has any other use but that it disengages us from the allurements of sense. In the state of future perfection, to which we all aspire, there will be pleasure without danger and security without restraint."

The princess was silent, and Rasselas, turning to the astronomer, asked him whether he could not delay her retreat by showing her something which she had not seen before.

[3] probatory "serving for trial" (*Dictionary*)

"Your curiosity," said the sage, "has been so general, and your pursuit of knowledge so vigorous, that novelties are not now very easily to be found: but what you can no longer procure from the living may be given by the dead. Among the wonders of this country are the catacombs, or the ancient repositories, in which the bodies of the earliest generations were lodged, and where, by the virtue of the gums which embalmed them, they yet remain without corruption."

"I know not," said Rasselas, "what pleasure the sight of the catacombs can afford; but, since nothing else is offered, I am resolved to view them, and shall place this with many other things which I have done because I would do something."

They hired a guard of horsemen, and the next day visited the catacombs. When they were about to descend into the sepulchral caves, "Pekuah," said the princess, "we are now again invading the habitations of the dead; I know that you will stay behind; let me find you safe when I return." "No, I will not be left," answered Pekuah; "I will go down between you and the prince."

They then all descended, and roved with wonder through the labyrinth of subterraneous passages, where the bodies were laid in rows on either side.

CHAPTER XLVIII

IMLAC DISCOURSES ON THE NATURE OF THE SOUL[1]

"What reason," said the prince, "can be given why the Egyptians should thus expensively preserve those carcasses which some nations consume with fire, others lay to mingle with the earth, and all agree to remove from their sight as soon as decent rites can be performed?"

[1] the Nature of the Soul the ideas presented in this chapter reflect arguments about the nature of the soul that were particularly spirited in England during the latter part of the seventeenth and the first part of the eighteenth century; see, for example, Locke's *Essay Concerning Human Understanding* (1690), Bk. IV, Chap. 3. In the *Dictionary,* Johnson defines *soul* as "The immaterial and immortal spirit of man"

"The original of ancient customs," said Imlac, "is commonly unknown; for the practice often continues when the cause has ceased; and concerning superstitious ceremonies it is vain to conjecture; for what reason did not dictate reason cannot explain. I have long believed that the practice of embalming arose only from tenderness to the remains of relations or friends, and to this opinion I am more inclined because it seems impossible that this care should have been general: had all the dead been embalmed, their repositories must in time have been more spacious than the dwellings of the living. I suppose only the rich or honourable were secured from corruption, and the rest left to the course of nature.

"But it is commonly supposed that the Egyptians believed the soul to live as long as the body continued undissolved, and therefore tried this method of eluding death."

"Could the wise Egyptians," said Nekayah, "think so grossly[2] of the soul? If the soul could once survive its separation, what could it afterwards receive or suffer from the body?"

"The Egyptians would doubtless think erroneously," said the astronomer, "in the darkness of heathenism and the first dawn of philosophy. The nature of the soul is still disputed amidst all our opportunities of clearer knowledge: some yet say that it may be material who, nevertheless, believe it to be immortal."

"Some," answered Imlac, "have indeed said that the soul is material, but I can scarcely believe that any man has thought it who knew how to think; for all the conclusions of reason enforce the immateriality of mind, and all the notices of sense and investigations of science concur to prove the unconsciousness of matter.[3]

"It was never supposed that cogitation is inherent in matter, or that every particle is a thinking being. Yet if any part of matter be devoid of thought, what part can we suppose to think? Matter can differ from matter only in form, density, bulk, motion, and direction of motion:

[2] grossly "without subtilty; without art; without delicacy; without refinement" (Dictionary)

[3] matter "body; substance extended" (Dictionary)

to which of these, however varied or combined, can consciousness be annexed? To be round or square, to be solid or fluid, to be great or little, to be moved slowly or swiftly one way or another, are modes of material existence, all equally alien from the nature of cogitation. If matter be once without thought, it can only be made to think by some new modification, but all the modifications which it can admit are equally unconnected with cogitative powers."

"But the materialists," [4] said the astronomer, "urge that matter may have qualities with which we are unacquainted."

"He who will determine," returned Imlac, "against that which he knows because there may be something which he knows not; he that can set hypothetical possibility against acknowledged certainty, is not to be admitted among reasonable beings. All that we know of matter is that matter is inert, senseless and lifeless; and if this conviction cannot be opposed but by referring us to something that we know not, we have all the evidence that human intellect can admit. If that which is known may be over ruled by that which is unknown, no being, not omniscient, can arrive at certainty."

"Yet let us not," said the astronomer, "too arrogantly limit the Creator's power."

"It is no limitation of omnipotence," replied the poet, "to suppose that one thing is not consistent with another, that the same proposition cannot be at once true and false, that the same number cannot be even and odd, that cogitation cannot be conferred on that which is created incapable of cogitation."

"I know not," said Nekayah, "any great use of this question. Does that immateriality which, in my opinion, you have sufficiently proved, necessarily include eternal duration?"

"Of immateriality," said Imlac, "our ideas are negative and therefore obscure. Immateriality seems to imply a natural power of perpetual duration as a consequence of exemption from all causes of decay: whatever perishes is

[4] materialists "one who denies spiritual substances" (*Dictionary*)

destroyed by the solution[5] of its contexture and separation of its parts; nor can we conceive how that which has no parts, and therefore admits no solution, can be naturally corrupted or impaired."

"I know not," said Rasselas, "how to conceive any thing without extension: what is extended must have parts, and you allow that whatever has parts may be destroyed."

"Consider your own conceptions," replied Imlac, "and the difficulty will be less. You will find substance without extension. An ideal form is no less real than material bulk: yet an ideal form has no extension. It is no less certain when you think on a pyramid that your mind possesses the idea of a pyramid than that the pyramid itself is standing. What space does the idea of a pyramid occupy more than the idea of a grain of corn? or how can either idea suffer laceration? As is the effect such is the cause; as thought is, such is the power that thinks; a power impassive[6] and indiscerptible." [7]

"But the Being," said Nekayah, "whom I fear to name, the Being which made the soul, can destroy it."

"He, surely, can destroy it," answered Imlac, "since, however unperishable, it receives from a superior nature its power of duration. That it will not perish by any inherent cause of decay, or principle of corruption, may be shown by philosophy; but philosophy can tell no more. That it will not be annihilated by him that made it, we must humbly learn from higher authority."

The whole assembly stood a while silent and collected. "Let us return," said Rasselas, "from this scene of mortality. How gloomy would be these mansions of the dead to him who did not know that he shall never die; that what now acts shall continue its agency, and what now thinks shall think on forever. Those that lie here stretched before us, the wise and the powerful of ancient times, warn us to remember the shortness of our present state:

[5] solution "disruption; breach; disjunction; separation" (*Dictionary*)

[6] impassive "exempt from the agency of external causes" (*Dictionary*)

[7] indiscerptible "not to be separated; incapable of being broken or destroyed by dissolution of parts" (*Dictionary*)

they were, perhaps, snatched away while they were busy, like us, in the choice of life."

"To me," said the princess, "the choice of life is become less important; I hope hereafter to think only on the choice of eternity."

They then hastened out of the caverns, and, under the protection of their guard, returned to Cairo.

CHAPTER XLIX

The Conclusion, in Which Nothing Is Concluded

It was now the time of the inundation of the Nile: a few days after their visit to the catacombs, the river began to rise.

They were confined to their house. The whole region being under water gave them no invitation to any excursions, and, being well supplied with materials for talk, they diverted themselves with comparisons of the different forms of life which they had observed, and with various schemes of happiness which each of them had formed.

Pekuah was never so much charmed with any place as the convent of St. Anthony, where the Arab restored her to the princess, and wished only to fill it with pious maidens, and to be made prioress of the order: she was weary of expectation and disgust, and would gladly be fixed in some unvariable state.

The princess thought that of all sublunary things knowledge was the best: She desired first to learn all sciences, and then purposed to found a college of learned women, in which she would preside, that, by conversing with the old and educating the young, she might divide her time between the acquisition and communication of wisdom, and raise up for the next age models of prudence and patterns of piety.

The prince desired a little kingdom in which he might administer justice in his own person, and see all the parts of government with his own eyes; but he could never fix the limits of his dominion, and was always adding to the number of his subjects.

Imlac and the astronomer were contented to be driven along the stream of life without directing their course to any particular port.

Of these wishes that they had formed they well knew that none could be obtained. They deliberated a while what was to be done, and resolved, when the inundation should cease, to return to Abyssinia.

FINIS

BIBLIOGRAPHY

LISTS OF WORKS BY AND ABOUT JOHNSON

Chapman, R. W., and Hazen, A. T., "Johnsonian Bibliography: A Supplement to Courtney," *Proceedings of the Oxford Bibliographical Society*, Vol. V (1939), pp. 119-66.

Clifford, J. L., *Johnsonian Studies, 1887-1950: A Survey and Bibliography* (Minneapolis, 1951).

———, and Greene, Donald J., "A Bibliography of Johnsonian Studies, 1950-1960," *Johnsonian Studies*, Magdi Wahba, ed. (Cairo, 1962), pp. 263-350.

Courtney, W. P., and Nichol Smith, D., *A Bibliography of Samuel Johnson* (Oxford, 1915).

Crane, R. S., *et al.*, "Samuel Johnson," *English Literature, 1660-1800: A Bibliography of Modern Studies Compiled for Philological Quarterly* (Vols. I-IV [1926-60]. Princeton, 1950, 1952, 1962).

JOHNSON'S OWN WRITINGS

Chapman, R. W., ed., *The History of Rasselas, Prince of Abyssinia* (Oxford, 1927).

Diaries, Prayers, and Annals, E. L. McAdam, Jr., and Donald and Mary Hyde, ed. (New Haven, 1958) [Vol. I of the Yale Edition of the *Works of Samuel Johnson.*]

Emerson, O. F., ed., *History of Rasselas, Prince of Abyssinia* (New York, 1895).

The Letters of Samuel Johnson, R. W. Chapman, ed., 3 vols. (Oxford, 1952).

The Poems of Samuel Johnson, D. Nichol Smith and E. L. McAdam, Jr., ed. (Oxford, 1941).

The Works of Samuel Johnson, LL.D., 11 vols. (Oxford, 1825) [To be gradually replaced by the Yale Edition of Johnson's Works.]

BIOGRAPHY AND CRITICISM

Bate, W. J., *The Achievement of Samuel Johnson* (New York, 1955).

Boswell, James, *The Life of Samuel Johnson, LL.D., Together with Boswell's Journal of a Tour to the Hebrides and Johnson's Diary of a Journey into North Wales,* G. B. Hill and L. F. Powell, eds., 6 vols. (Oxford, 1934, 1950) [The standard edition of the *Life*].

Bronson, B. H., *Johnson and Boswell: Three Essays* (Berkeley, 1944).

Clifford, J. L., *Young Sam Johnson* (New York, 1955).

Greene, D. J., *The Politics of Samuel Johnson* (New Haven, 1960).

Hagstrum, J. H., *Samuel Johnson's Literary Criticism* (Minneapolis, 1952).

Johnsonian Miscellanies, G. B. Hill, ed., 2 vols. (Oxford, 1897).

Keast, W. R., "The Theoretical Foundations of Samuel Johnson's Criticism," *Critics and Criticism, Ancient and Modern,* R. S. Crane, ed. (Chicago, 1952), pp. 389-407.

Kolb, G. J., "The Structure of *Rasselas*," *PMLA,* Vol. LXVI (1951), pp. 698-717.

———, "The 'Paradise' in Abyssinia and the 'Happy Valley' in *Rasselas*," *Modern Philology,* Vol. LVI (1958), pp. 10-16.

Krutch, J. W., *Samuel Johnson* (New York, 1944).

New Light on Dr. Johnson, F. W. Hilles, ed. (New Haven, 1959).

Nichol Smith, D., "Johnson and Boswell," *Cambridge History of English Literature,* Vol. X, pp. 157-94 (Cambridge, 1913).

Raleigh, Walter, *Six Essays on Johnson* (Oxford, 1910).

Sherburn, George, "Dr. Johnson," *The Restoration and Eighteenth Century (1660-1789)* (A Literary History of England, Vol. III) (New York, 1948), pp. 989-1004.

Wimsatt, W. K., Jr., *Philosophic Words: A Study of Style and Meaning in the Rambler and Dictionary by Johnson* (New Haven, 1948).

———, *The Prose Style of Samuel Johnson* (New Haven, 1941).

BACKGROUND OF JOHNSON'S LIFE

Turberville, A. S., ed., *Johnson's England,* 2 vols. (Oxford, 1933).